Daddy-Long-Legs
長腿叔叔

Original Author   Jean Webster
Adaptors   Louise Benette / David Hwang
Illustrator   An Ji-Yeon

WORDS
450

MP3

Let's Enjoy Masterpieces!

All the beautiful fairy tales and masterpieces that you have encountered during your childhood remain as warm memories in your adulthood. This time, let's indulge in the world of masterpieces through English. You can enjoy the depth and beauty of original works, which you can't enjoy through Chinese translations.

The stories are easy for you to understand because of your familiarity with them. When you enjoy reading, your ability to understand English will also rapidly improve.

This series of *Let's Enjoy Masterpieces* is a special reading comprehension booster program, devised to improve reading comprehension for beginners whose command of English is not satisfactory, or who are elementary, middle, and high school students. With this program, you can enjoy reading masterpieces in English with fun and efficiency.

This carefully planned program is composed of 5 levels, from the beginner level of 350 words to the intermediate and advanced levels of 1,000 words. With this program's level-by-level system, you are able to read famous texts in English and to savor the true pleasure of the world's language.

The program is well conceived, composed of reader-friendly explanations of English expressions and grammar, quizzes to help the student learn vocabulary and understand the meaning of the texts, and fabulous illustrations that adorn every page. In addition, with our "Guide to Listening," not only is reading comprehension enhanced but also listening comprehension skills are highlighted.

In the audio recording of the book, texts are vividly read by professional American actors. The texts are rewritten, according to the levels of the readers by an expert editorial staff of native speakers, on the basis of standard American English with the ministry of education recommended vocabulary. Therefore, it will be of great help even for all the students that want to learn English.

Please indulge yourself in the fun of reading and listening to English through *Let's Enjoy Masterpieces*.

珍·韋伯斯特

Jean Webster
(1876-1916)

American author Jean Webster, christened Alice Jane Chandler Webster, was born of a rich family in Fredonia, New York in 1876. She was a relative, on her mother's side, of the famous American author Mark Twain. When she attended the Lady Jane Grey boarding school, her roommate was a girl named Alice. To avoid any confusion, Alice Webster changed her name to Jean Webster. In 1901 she graduated from Vassar College with the double majors of English literature and economics.

As an undergraduate, Jean Webster wrote a number of stories for Vassar's literary magazine and for Vassar's newspaper. She was concerned about orphan asylum reform as well as prison reform, which also provided a backdrop for her novels.

Her first collection of short stories, *When Patty Went to College*, was written when she was in school. It was published in 1903 and was successful. After that, *Daddy-Long-Legs* (1912) and *Dear Enemy* (1915) were published, and she became famous as a writer. Her witty novels have a good reputation and are written in a style that is often described as American idealism.

She married in 1915. Soon after her daughter was born in 1916, Jean Webster died as a result of birth complications. Sadly, Jean Webster's early death deprived her of the chance to fully enjoy her life and to write more great novels. Although her life was short, her books are still read today and continue to inspire many women around the world.

Daddy-Long-Legs

Jerusha Abbott, an orphan at birth, has had difficult times in the John Grier Orphanage. She has a talent for writing and is full of dreams. Now a wealthy anonymous benefactor has offered to put her through college. All he asks for in return is that she writes him one detailed letter about her experiences in college per month. Jerusha gives this strange but kind man the nickname of "*Daddy-Long Legs*."

Daddy-Long-Legs is a collection of the letters that she wrote to her benefactor. There were a lot of novels in the past that were written in the form of letters. However, this novel is unusual, because it is both funny and touching. It is vividly written because every character has a unique personality. It is particularly striking in the description of Jerusha's smart and cheerful personality. However, the true merit of this book is in the showing of benevolence, humanity, and equality among people.

HOW TO USE THIS BOOK
本書使用說明

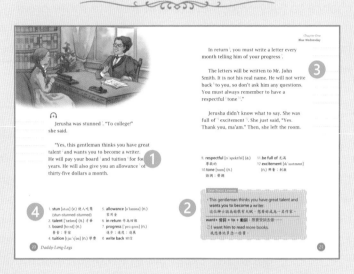

1 Original English texts

It is easy to understand the meaning of the text, because the text is divided phrase by phrase and sentence by sentence.

2 Explanation of the vocabulary

The words and expressions that include vocabulary above the elementary level are clearly defined.

3 Response notes

Spaces are included in the book so you can take notes about what you don't understand or what you want to remember.

4 One point lesson

In-depth analyses of major grammar points and expressions help you to understand sentences with difficult grammar.

∩ *Audio Recording*

In the audio recording, native speakers narrate the texts in standard American English. By combining the written words and the audio recording, you can listen to English with great ease.

Audio books have been popular in Britain and America for many decades. They allow the listener to experience the proper word pronunciation and sentence intonation that add important meaning and drama to spoken English. Students will benefit from listening to the recording twenty or more times.

After you are familiar with the text and recording, listen once more with your eyes closed to check your listening comprehension. Finally, after you can listen with your eyes closed and understand every word and every sentence, you are then ready to mimic the native speaker.

Then you should make a recording by reading the text yourself. Then play both recordings to compare your oral skills with those of a native speaker.

HOW TO IMPROVE
READING ABILITY

如何增進英文閱讀能力

① *Catch key words*

Read the key words in the sentences and practice catching the gist of the meaning of the sentence. You might question how working with a few important words could enhance your reading ability. However, it's quite effective. If you continue to use this method, you will find out that the key words and your knowledge of people and situations enables you to understand the sentence.

② *Divide long sentences*

Read in chunks of meaning, dividing sentences into meaningful chunks of information. In the book, chunks are arranged in sentences according to meaning. If you consider the sentences backwards or grammatically, your reading speed will be slow and you will find it difficult to listen to English.

You are ready to move to a more sophisticated level of comprehension when you find that narrowly focusing on chunks is irritating. Instead of considering the chunks, you will make it a habit to read the sentence from the beginning to the end to figure out the meaning of the whole.

❸ Make inferences and assumptions

Making inferences and assumptions is part of your ability. If you don't know, try to guess the meaning of the words. Although you don't know all the words in context, don't go straight to the dictionary. Developing an ability to make inferences in the context is important.

The first way to figure out the meaning of a word is from its context. If you cannot make head or tail out of the meaning of a word, look at what comes before or after it. Ask yourself what can happen in such a situation. Make your best guess as to the word's meaning. Then check the explanations of the word in the book or look up the word in a dictionary.

❹ Read a lot and reread the same book many times

There is no shortcut to mastering English. Only if you do a lot of reading will you make your way to the summit. Read fun and easy books with an average of less than one new word per page. Try to immerse yourself in English as often as you can.

Spend time "swimming" in English. Language learning research has shown that immersing yourself in English will help you improve your English, even though you may not be aware of what you're learning.

CONTENTS

Before You Read

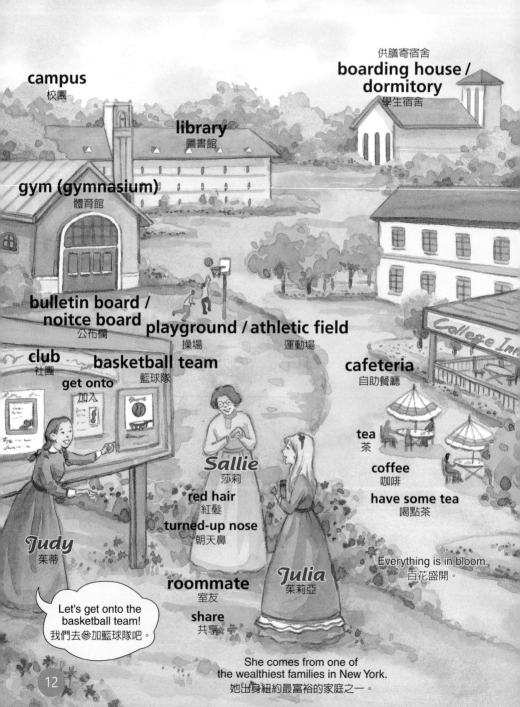

campus
校園

boarding house /
dormitory
供膳寄宿舍
學生宿舍

library
圖書館

gym (gymnasium)
體育館

bulletin board /
noitce board
公布欄

playground / athletic field
操場   運動場

club
社團

get onto
加入

basketball team
籃球隊

cafeteria
自助餐廳

College Inn

tea
茶

coffee
咖啡

have some tea
喝點茶

Sallie
莎莉

red hair
紅髮

turned-up nose
朝天鼻

Judy
茱蒂

Everything is in bloom.
百花盛開。

roommate
室友

Julia
茱莉亞

Let's get onto the
basketball team!
我們去參加籃球隊吧。

share
共享

She comes from one of
the wealthiest families in New York.
她出身紐約最富裕的家庭之一。

12

January 一月

Happy New Year!
新年快樂！

February 二月

subject 科目
mathematics 數學
chemistry 化學
physiology 生理學
geometry 幾何學
Latin 拉丁文

March 三月

Short Story Contest
短篇小說比賽

April 四月

Sports Day
運動日

Cheerful Parade
歡欣鼓舞的遊行

May 五月

The campus is gorgeous in May.
五月時校園會很美。

June 六月

Final Exam
期末考

Graduation
畢業

July 七月   August 八月

Wonderful Vacation at Lock Willow!
在細柳湖的美好假期。

September 九月

new semester 新學期
freshman 新生
sophomore 二年級生
junior 三年級生
senior 四年級生

October 十月

Class President Election
班代選舉
run for
競選

November 十一月

get onto the basketball team
加入籃球隊

December 十二月

Merry Christmas!
聖誕快樂！

Chapter One

🎧 Blue[1] Wednesday

On the first Wednesday of every month, the trustees[2] of the John Grier Orphanage[3] came to visit.

Jerusha Abbott hated these days the most. She was the oldest orphan[4] in the home[5]. She had the responsibility[6] to make sure[7] everything was completely[8] clean. She also had to clean every one of the ninety-seven orphans.

1. **blue** [blu:] (a.) 憂鬱的
2. **trustee** [trʌsˋti:] (n.) 基金會等的受託人；大學等機構的董事
3. **orphanage** [ˋɔ:rfənɪdʒ] (n.) 孤兒院
4. **orphan** [ˋɔ:rfən] (n.) 孤兒
5. **home** (n.) 此指孤兒院及中途之家
6. **responsibility** [ˌrɪspɑ:nsəˋbɪləti] (n.) 責任

Today was one of those days. Now the day was over and she was sitting down, thinking about the day.

Mrs. Lippett, the matron[9], had kept Jerusha busy all day long[10]. Jerusha looked out the window and watched the trustees driving through the orphanage gates. She was dreaming of[11] driving away in a similar[12] car when she heard a familiar voice.

7. **make sure** 確保
8. **completely** [kəm`pli:tli] (adv.) 完全地;整個地
9. **matron** [`meɪtrən] (n.) 女院長
10. **all day long** 整天
11. **dream of** 夢想
12. **similar** [`sɪmɪlər] (a.) 相似的;類似的

15

"Jerusha! You have to go to the office now!"
It was Tommy Dillon. He was another orphan
in the home.

A feeling of panic[1] went through[2] Jerusha's
body. "What did I do wrong?" she thought.
"Weren't the sandwiches tasty[3] enough?
Oh my![4] Was one of the orphans rude[5]?"

She was walking to Mrs. Lippett's office
when she saw the back of a man. He cast[6] a
shadow[7] on the hall[8].
He had very long legs and arms and his
shadow looked just like a daddy-long-legs
spider[9].

Jerusha entered the office. Mrs. Lippett
immediately spoke, "Jerusha! I have news for
you. Did you see the gentleman who has just
left?"
"I only saw his back," Jerusha replied[10].

1. **panic** [ˋpænɪk] (n.)
   恐慌；慌亂
2. **go through** 貫穿；穿過
3. **tasty** [ˋteɪstɪ] (a.)
   好吃的；可口的
4. **Oh my!**
   唉呀；哇；咦（表示驚訝、
   疑惑的嘆詞）
5. **rude** [ru:d] (a.) 無禮的

6. **cast** [kæst] (v.) 投射
   (cast-cast-cast)
7. **shadow** [ˋʃædoʊ] (n.) 影子
8. **hall** [hɔ:l] (n.) 門廳；走廊
9. **daddy-long-legs spider**
   幽靈蜘蛛（一種常見的長腳
   蜘蛛）
10. **reply** [rɪˋplaɪ] (v.)
    回答；回覆

"He is one of our most important trustees. He told me not to tell you his name. He doesn't want you to know it."

"Why is she telling me this?" Jerusha thought to herself[1].

Mrs. Lippett continued, "Do you remember Charles Benton and Henry Freize? Well, this gentleman sent them and other boys to college[2]. Until now[3], he has only chosen[4] boys.

1. **think to oneself** 在心裡想
2. **college** [`ka:lɪdʒ] (n.) 大學；學院
3. **until now** 直到現在
4. **choose** [tʃu:z] (v.) 選擇 (choose-chose-chosen)
5. **meeting** [`mi:tɪŋ] (n.) 會議
6. **discuss** [dɪ`skʌs] (v.) 討論
7. **normally** [`nɔ:rməli] (adv.) 正常地；一般情況地
8. **be expected to . . .** 被期待應……
9. **consider** [kən`sɪdər] (v.) 考慮；斟酌
10. **excellent** [`eksələnt] (a.) 出色的；優異的
11. **grade** [greɪd] (n.) 成績
12. **offer** [`a:fər] (v.) 提供

He does not really like girls. However, at the meeting[5] today, you were discussed[6].

Now you are too old to stay at the orphanage. Normally[7], you would be expected[8] to work, but considering[9] your excellent[10] grades[11], especially in English, this gentleman has offered[12] to send you to college."

One Point Lesson

Until now, he **has** only **chosen** boys.
在這之前，他只挑選了男生。

---

have + 過去分詞：為完成式，此處表示「已經發生的事情」，類似中文裡常用的「了」。

e.g. **I have studied** English for five years.
我學英文有五年了。

 4

Jerusha was stunned[1]. "To college!" she said.

"Yes, this gentleman thinks you have great talent[2] and wants you to become a writer. He will pay your board[3] and tuition[4] for four years. He will also give you an allowance[5] of thirty-five dollars a month.

1. **stun** [stʌn] (v.) 使人吃驚 (stun-stunned-stunned)
2. **talent** [ˋtælənt] (n.) 才華
3. **board** [bɔːrd] (n.) 餐食；寄宿
4. **tuition** [tjuːˋɪʃən] (n.) 學費

5. **allowance** [əˋlaʊəns] (n.) 零用金
6. **in return** 作為回報
7. **progress** [ˋprɑːgres] (n.) 進步；進度；進展
8. **write back** 回信

In return[6], you must write a letter every month telling him of your progress[7].

The letters will be written to Mr. John Smith. It is not his real name. He will not write back[8] to you, so don't ask him any questions. You must always remember to have a respectful[9] tone[10]."

Jerusha didn't know what to say. She was full of[11] excitement[12]. She just said, "Yes. Thank you, ma'am." Then, she left the room.

9. **respectful** [rɪ`spɛktfəl] (a.)
   尊敬的
10. **tone** [toʊn] (n.)
   語調；聲調

11. **be full of** 充滿
12. **excitement** [ɪk`saɪtmənt]
   (n.) 興奮；刺激

One Point Lesson

This gentleman thinks you have great talent and wants you to become a writer.
這位紳士認為妳很有天賦，想要妳成為一名作家。

want + 受詞 + **to** + 動詞：想要受詞去做……

e.g. I want him to read more books.
我想要他多念一些書。

215 Fergussen Hall
September 24th

🎧 5

Dear Kind-Trustee-Who-Sends-Orphans-to-College,

I am finally here at college. I am so amazed[1] by everything here. I still get lost[2] whenever[3] I go out. Later[4], I will give you a better description[5] of the place.

I don't begin classes until Monday, but I wanted to write a letter immediately. I've never written many letters before so it seems[6] strange to be writing one now.

Before I left yesterday morning, Mrs. Lippett told me to always be Very Respectful to you, but how can I be when I don't know you?

1. **amazed** [ə`meɪzd] (a.)
   驚歎的；驚異的
2. **get lost** 迷路；迷失
   (get-got-gotten)
3. **whenever** [wen`evər]
   (conj.) 無論何時
4. **later** [`leɪtər] (adv.)
   稍晚地；較晚地
5. **description** [dɪ`skrɪpʃən]
   (n.) 描述；描寫
6. **seem** [si:m] (v.) 似乎

● I've never **written** many letters before so it seems strange to be writing one now.

　我以前從未寫過什麼信，所以現在寫信感覺似乎很奇怪。

---

have + 過去分詞：此處表示「到現在為止，已經完成或尚未完成的事」，後面可與 ever 或 never 連用。

● I have **never seen** the picture. 我從未見過這張照片。

　I have **read** this book once. 我讀過一次這本書。

I only know three things about you:

    1. You are tall.
    2. You are rich.
    3. You hate[1] girls.

Why do I have to call you Mr. John Smith?
If I called you Dear Mr. Girl Hater or Dear Mr.
Rich Man, that wouldn't be very nice.

1. **hate** [heɪt] (v.) 討厭；厭惡
2. **What about . . . ?**
   對於⋯⋯的看法呢？
3. **mind** [maɪnd] (v.) 介意
4. **all right with** *sb*
   對某人來說沒關係的

But what about[2] Dear Daddy-Long-Legs?
Do you mind[3]? I hope it's all right with[4] you.
It's just a private[5] pet name[6]. We won't tell
Mrs. Lippett.

There goes the evening bell[7]! Lights out!
Good night, Daddy-Long-Legs.

Yours most respectfully[8],
Jerusha Abbott.

5. **private** [ˋpraɪvət] (a.)
   私人的；私密的
6. **pet name** 暱稱
7. **evening bell** 晚鐘
8. **Yours most respectfully**
   最尊敬您的

A Fill in the blanks with the given words.

rude	have	respectful	written

1 You must always remember to have a
_____ tone.

2 Oh my! Was one of the orphans _____?

3 I _____ never _____ many
letters before.

B True or False.

T F **1** Jerusha imagined herself dressed in the
finest clothes at the end of the day.

T F **2** The man Jerusha saw had very long arms
and legs.

T F **3** The man decided to send Jerusha to
college because he liked girls.

T F **4** Jerusha felt uncomfortable when she was
writing a letter to someone she didn't
know.

C Choose the best answer to each question.

1 Why did Jerusha hate the first Wednesday of every month?

(a) She had to do a lot of homework.

(b) She was always punished on those days.

(c) She was extremely busy all day long.

2 Which is not a condition of Jerusha going to college?

(a) She must write to Mr. John Smith.

(b) She receives thirty-five dollars a month.

(c) She must ask Mr. John Smith many questions.

D Fill in the blanks with the given words Remember to change the tense of verbs accordingly.

> watch   keep   be finished   hear   look

Now the blue Wednesday **1** _____ and Jerusha was sitting down, thinking about the day. Mrs. Lippett had **2** _____ her busy all day long. She **3** _____ out the window and **4** _____ the trustees driving through the orphanage gates. She was dreaming of driving away in a similar car when she **5** _____ a familiar voice.

· Chapter Two ·

🎧[7] College Begins

October 1st

Dear Daddy-Long-Legs,

I am so happy to be here. I love you for sending me here. It is an amazing[1] place.

My room is high in a tower[2]. There are two girls here with me. One is Sallie McBride who has red hair and a turned-up nose[3].
The other is Julia Rutledge Pendleton. She comes from[4] one of the wealthiest[5] families in New York.

I am so happy to have my own room after having had to share one with many others.

This letter will be very short today.
I'm hoping to get onto[6] the basketball team.
I know I'm not tall, but I am very quick.
I can move faster than any of the other girls.
I'll write you a longer letter next time.
Wish me luck for the basketball team!

Yours always[7],
Jerusha Abbot

1. **amazing** [ə`meɪzɪŋ] (a.)
   令人驚異的

2. **tower** [`taʊər] (n.) 塔；塔樓

3. **turned-up nose** 上翹的鼻子

4. **come from** 出身自

5. **wealthy** [`welθi] (a.)
   富有的

6. **get onto . . .**
   為……的一員；加入……

7. **Yours always** 您永遠的

Dear Daddy-Long-Legs,

I've furnished[1] my room. I bought some yellow curtains[2], brown cushions[3], a mahogany[4] desk, a cane[5] chair and a brown rug[6]. It looks so much better now.

I really like where I am living. I really like Sallie McBride, but I don't like Julia Rutledge Pendleton. She never makes an effort to[7] be friendly to me.

1. **furnish** [ˋfɜːrnɪʃ] (v.)
   裝潢；陳設；裝備家具
2. **curtain** [ˋkɜːrtən] (n.) 窗簾
3. **cushion** [ˋkuʃən] (n.) 靠墊

4. **mahogany** [məˋhɑːgəni] (a.) 紅木做的
5. **cane** [keɪn] (n.) 藤
6. **rug** [rʌg] (n.) 小地毯

I am studying many things like geometry[8], physiology[9], French, Latin[10] and English, which is my favorite.

In fact, for my last English paper[11], my teacher said it was amazingly original[12]. Isn't that great considering I grew up in a place which does not encourage[13] originality[14]?

7. **make an effort to**
付出努力；花心力

8. **geometry** [dʒiˋɑ:mətri] (n.)
幾何學

9. **physiology** [ˌfiziˋɑ:lədʒi]
(n.) 生理學

10. **Latin** [ˋlætɪn] (n.) 拉丁文

11. **paper** [ˋpeɪpər] (n.)
報告；論文

12. **original** [əˋrɪdʒɪnəl] (a.)
原創的

13. **encourage** [ɪnˋkɜ:rɪdʒ] (v.)
鼓勵

14. **originality** [əˌrɪdʒɪˋnæləti]
(n.) 創意；原創力

One Point Lesson

● Isn't that great **considering** I grew up in a place which does not encourage originality?
想想我是在一個不鼓勵原創性的地方長大，所以老師那樣說不是太棒了嗎？

分詞構句：如果子句與主句的主詞相同，子句的動詞可改用分詞形式，並省略主詞。

e.g **After we finished** our work, we went to a restaurant.
→ **Finishing** our work, we went to a restaurant.
我們完成工作後，就去上館子了。
→子句的主詞省略，改用分詞構句。

🎧 9

I know, I shouldn't say bad things about[1] the orphanage. You know, no one knows I grew up in an orphanage. I don't want to be different from[2] any of the other girls although I told Sallie McBride that my mother and father are dead.

I told her a kind, old gentleman is sending me to college. Now that's true, isn't it?

Oh, by the way[3], I've also changed my name to[4] Judy, so please call me Judy from now on[5].

Yours ever,
Judy (formerly[6] Jerusha) Abbott

1. **say bad things about . . .**
   說……的壞話
2. **be different from . . .**
   與……不同
3. **by the way** 對了（口語）
4. **change A to B** 把 A 改為 B
5. **from now on** 從今以後
6. **formerly** [ˋfɔːrmərli] (adv.)
   原先地；之前地

October 25th

Dear Daddy-Long-Legs,

Hooray![7] I got onto the basketball team. Julia Pendleton didn't, however!

I have bruises[8] all over[9] my body. I love college so much. Everything is just getting better and better.

Judy at Basket Ball

I know I am not supposed to[10] ask you any questions but I have just one. What does a tall, rich, generous[11] man who hates girls look like?

Please answer this question. It is important[12] to me.

Yours,
Judy Abbott.

7. **hooray** [huˋreɪ] (int.)
   萬歲；加油
8. **bruise** [bruːz] (n.) 瘀青
9. **all over** 遍佈
10. **be supposed to . . .**
   （被認為）應當去做……

11. **generous** [ˋdʒeɪnərəs] (a.)
   慷慨的；寬大的
12. **important** [ɪmˋpɔːrtənt] (a.)
   重要的

33

Dear Daddy-Long-Legs,

You never answered my question.
ARE YOU BALD[1]? I have an idea of[2] what you
look like except[3] your head. I can't decide
whether[4] you have black hair, white
hair or salt and pepper hair[5].
Maybe you have none at all[6].

I made a portrait[7] of you.
I think you look like this:
(add[8] picture)
You seem to be just an angry
old man.

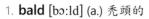

1. **bald** [bɔːld] (a.) 禿頭的
2. **have an idea of**
   對……有概念；想法
3. **except** [ɪkˋsept] (prep.)
   除了
4. **whether** *A* **or** *B*
   A 或 B 兩者之一
5. **salt and pepper hair**
   通常指男性黑灰摻雜的頭髮
6. **have none at all** 一點也沒有
7. **portrait** [ˋpɔːrtrɪt] (n.)
   肖像畫
8. **add** [æd] (v.) 添加；附加

There are so many books that I need to read. All of the other girls have read all of the books I need to read.

Christmas holidays[9] begin next week. Another girl and I will be the only ones staying behind[10]. I plan to do lots of[11] reading for the whole three weeks of it. It will be wonderful.

Yours always,
Judy

P. S.[12] Please tell me what you look like. Ask your secretary[13] to send a telegram[14] with either[15]:
    1. Mr. Smith is quite bald.
    Or 2. Mr. Smith is not bald.
    Or 3. Mr. Smith has white hair.

9. **Christmas holidays**
   耶誕假期
10. **stay behind** 留下來不走
11. **lots of** 許多
12. **P.S.** 附記（= postscript）
13. **secretary** [ˋsɛkrətəri] (n.)
    秘書
14. **telegram** [ˋtɛləgræm] (n.)
    電報
15. **either** [ˋaɪðə] (pron.)
    兩者之一

Exact Date Unknown[1]

Dear Daddy-Long-Legs,

It is snowing here and everything is blanketed[2] in white.

Thank you for[3] the Christmas present. The five gold pieces[4] were a big surprise especially considering that you have done so much for me.

Do you want to know what I bought? I bought a silver watch so I will always be on time[5], five hundred sheets of yellow manuscript paper[6] (for when I become an author[7]), a dictionary of synonyms[8] (to improve[9] my vocabulary[10]).

1. **unknown** [ʌnˋnoʊn] (a.) 未知的；不明的
2. **blanket** [ˋblæŋkɪt] (v.) 如毯子一般覆蓋
3. **thank you for** 為……感謝你
4. **piece** [pi:s] (n.) 舊時英美使用的錢幣（coin）
5. **be on time** 準時
6. **manuscript paper** 稿紙
7. **author** [ˋɔ:θər] (n.) 作者
8. **synonym** [ˋsɪnənɪm] (n.) 同義詞
9. **improve** [ɪmˋpru:v] (v.) 改善；增進
10. **vocabulary** [voʊˋkæbjələri] (n.) 字彙
11. **in two days** 兩天內
12. **know of** (know-knew-known) 知道……；認識……

Thank you so much for all of these presents. The holidays will be over in two days[11]. It will be good to see everyone. It has become a little lonely here.

Thank you for everything you have done for me.

Yours with love,
Judy

P.S. I hope you don't mind me sending love. I need someone to love and you are the only person I know of[12].

◆ **It is snowing here and everything is blanketed in white.** 這裡在下雪，萬物覆蓋著一片白。

it：講天氣、天色時，英文中皆以 it 來表示。但是在中文中通常會加以省略。

◐ **It is getting dark outside**
屋外（天色）漸漸暗了。

🎧 12

Sunday

Dear Daddy-Long-Legs,

First, I have some great news. Jerusha Abbott has become an author. My poem[1], "From My Tower" will appear in the February Monthly[2]. I will send you a copy[3] of it. Isn't that great?

I've been doing so many other things as well[4]. I've learned how to skate. I can now skate around without falling down[5].

1. **poem** [ˋpouəm] (n.) 詩
2. **monthly** [ˋmʌnθli] (n.) 月刊
3. **copy** [ˋkɑːpi] (n.) 本；份
4. **as well** 也
5. **fall down** 跌落

Also, in gym[6], I can slide down[7] a rope from the top of the gym and I learned to vault[8] a bar[9] three feet and six inches high.

It was very scary[10] at first[11], but now I do everything very easily.

Well, I have some bad news, too. I hope you are in a good mood[12]. I failed[13] mathematics[14] and Latin. But I'm being tutored[15] in them now. Please forgive[16] me. I promise[17] I will not fail again.

6. **gym** 體育館
   (= gymnasium)
7. **slide down** 滑下
8. **vault** [vɔːlt] (v.)（以手或竿子支撐）跳躍；翻越
9. **bar** [bɑːr] (n.) 槓；桿
10. **scary** [`skeri] (adv.) 可怕的；恐怖的
11. **at first** 起初；一開始
12. **in a good mood** 心情很好
13. **fail** [feɪl] (v.) 沒通過
14. **mathematics** [ˌmæθə`mætɪks] (n.) 數學（簡稱 math）
15. **tutor** [`tuːtər] (v.) 家教或助教個別指導
16. **forgive** [fərˋgɪv] (v.) 原諒 (forgive-forgave-forgiven)
17. **promise** [`prɑːmɪs] (v.) 答應；保證；允諾

I've learned so many other things, and I've read seventeen novels[1] and lots of poetry[2].

Mathematics and Latin aren't everything!

Yours,
Judy

NEWS of the MONTH

Judy learns to skate

And to vault a bar.

She receives two flunk notes
and sheds
many tears

But Promises to study
HARD

May 27th

Dear Daddy-Long-Legs,

I just received[3] a letter from Mrs. Lippett. She told me I could go back to the orphanage and work during the summer.

I hate the John Grier Home. I would prefer to[4] die[5].

Yours most honestly[6],
Jerusha Abbott.

1. **novel** [`nɑ:vəl] (n.) 小說
2. **poetry** [`pouətri] (n.)
   詩的通稱
3. **receive** [rɪ`si:v] (v.)
   接獲；收到
4. **prefer to** 偏好於
5. **die** [daɪ] (v.) 死
6. **honestly** [`ɑ:nəstli] (adv.)
   誠實地

A Match the words with the descriptions.

1 furnish • • **a** a place where children with
no parents live

2 bald • • **b** a bluish-green color on
the skin

3 orphanage • • **c** to put furniture in a room
or house

4 portrait • • **d** uniqueness

5 originality • • **e** having no hair on the head

6 bruise • • **f** a picture or painting of
a person

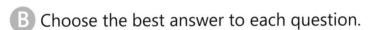

B Choose the best answer to each question.

1 Why does Jerusha dislike Julia Pendelton?

(a) Because she is so beautiful.

(b) Because she doesn't make efforts to be friendly.

(c) Because she knows that Jerusha is an orphan.

2 What does Jerusha want to know about Daddy most?

(a) Whom he loves.

(b) How old he is.

(c) What he looks like.

C True or False.

T F ① Jerusha was quite tall and very quick.

T F ② Jerusha really missed her life at the orphanage.

T F ③ Jerusha told Sallie that a man paid for her college.

T F ④ Jerusha doesn't like reading books at all.

T F ⑤ Jerusha was happy to get Christmas presents.

D Rearrange the following sentences in chronological order.

① Jerusha got onto the basketball team.

② Jerusha failed math and Latin.

③ Jerusha started living on campus.

④ She learned how to skate.

⑤ Jerusha bought a silver watch.

⑥ Jerusha decorated her room.

_____ ⇨ _____ ⇨ _____ ⇨ _____ ⇨ _____ ⇨ _____

Before You Read

The View of Lock Willow
細柳湖的景色

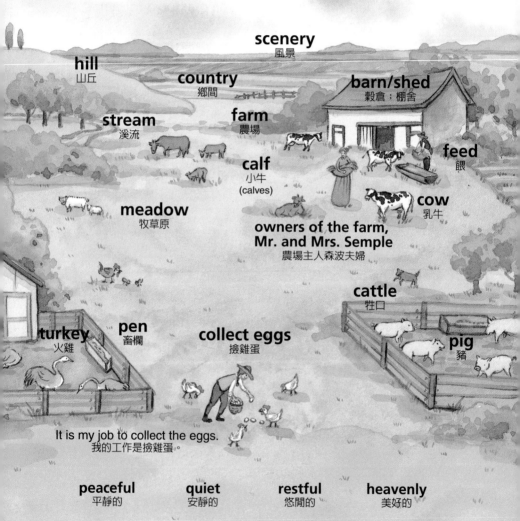

scenery
風景

hill
山丘

country
鄉間

barn/shed
穀倉：棚舍

stream
溪流

farm
農場

feed
餵

calf
小牛
(calves)

cow
乳牛

meadow
牧草原

owners of the farm, Mr. and Mrs. Semple
農場主人森波夫婦

cattle
牲口

turkey
火雞

pen
畜欄

collect eggs
撿雞蛋

pig
豬

It is my job to collect the eggs.
我的工作是撿雞蛋。

peaceful
平靜的

quiet
安靜的

restful
悠閒的

heavenly
美好的

It is the most wonderful, heavenly place.
那是一個極其美好的地方

Amazing New York
令人嘆為觀止的紐約

I am here in New York now!
我人現在在紐約！

city
城市

urban
市區

buildings
建築物

theater
劇院

play
舞台劇

actor/actress
演員／女演員

Hamlet
哈姆雷特

restaurant
餐廳

hotel
飯店

shops
商店

go shopping
逛街購物

waiter/waitress
侍者／女服務生

try on
試穿

street
街道

traffic
交通

a bunch of flowers
一束花

meal
餐

order
點菜

Master Jervie
喆維斯少爺

I ordered fish, but I didn't know which fork to use.
我點了魚，不知要用哪根叉子吃。

busy
忙碌的

exciting
令人興奮的

confusing
令人困惑的

sidewalk/pavement
人行道

Everything is so wonderful but so confusing at the same time.
每一樣東西都令人驚奇又感到困惑。

Chapter Three

Master¹ Jervie

🎧 14

May 30th

Dear Daddy-Long-Legs,

This campus² is gorgeous³ in May.
Everything is in bloom⁴. Everyone is outside
enjoying the fine weather.

We have examinations soon, but no one is
thinking about them. Vacation will be here
soon! I am so happy, too! I am going to work
really hard this summer and become a great
author.

---

1. **master** [`mæstər] (n.)
   大爺；爵爺（稱呼有爵位或
   地位的男士）

2. **campus** [`kæmpəs] (n.) 校園

I have some other news for you. I have been spending time with[5] a very nice man. He is a man of superior[6] quality[7]. He is Mr. Jervis Pendleton of the house of Julia. He is her very tall uncle.

He was in town on business[8] and decided to visit Julia. She was in class[9], so he asked me to walk around the campus with him.

3. **gorgeous** [`gɔ:rdʒəs] (a.)
   迷人的；美麗的；燦爛的
4. **in bloom** 盛開
5. **spend time with** *sb*
   與某人共度時光
   (spend-spent-spent)

6. **superior** [sʊ:`pɪriər] (a.)
   優越的；極好的
7. **quality** [`kwɑ:ləti] (n.)
   品質；特性
8. **on business** 處理公事
9. **in class** 上課

He is not like the other Pendletons at all.
He is such a¹ kind man. He is tall and thin with
the funniest smile.

I felt very comfortable with² him.
We walked all around the campus and then
had tea and muffins³ and marmalade⁴ and ice
cream and cake at the College Inn⁵. It was the
best time.

1. **such a + *adj.* + *n.***
   如此……的一個……
2. **feel comfortable with *sb***
   和某人在一起時覺得很自在
3. **muffin** [ˈmʌfɪn] (n.)
   馬芬麵包；英式小鬆餅
4. **marmalade** [ˈmɑːrməleɪd]
   (n.)（橘子或檸檬）果醬
5. **inn** [ɪn] (n.) 餐廳
6. **catch the train** 趕火車
7. **be angry with *sb***
   對某人生氣
8. **extremely** [ɪkˈstriːmli]
   (adv.) 極端地；非常地
9. **each** [iːtʃ] (adv.) 各自地

But then he had to run and catch his train[6]. Julia was angry with[7] me for taking him the whole time.

It seems he is an extremely[8] wealthy uncle. And this morning, Julia, Sallie and myself all received surprises. A box of chocolates each[9]!

I really don't feel like an orphan anymore!

Yours always,
Judy

One Point Lesson

• He is not like **the other Pendletons** at all.
他一點也不像潘鐸頓家族的其他人。

the + 姓氏 s：表示家族，或家族中的一部分人。
如：the Kennedys，甘酒迪家族。
e.g. We had dinner with **the Kims**.
我們跟金姆一家人（或夫婦，或兄弟，或父子……）
吃飯。

49

June 9th

Dear Daddy-Long-Legs,

My examinations are finally over.

I'm excited about spending three months on a farm[1]. Thank you so much for sending me there instead of[2] the orphanage.

I've never been on a farm before but I know I will love Lock Willow.

Yours ever,
Judy

Saturday night

Dear Daddy-Long-Legs,

I am here at the farm. It is the most wonderful, heavenly[3] place.

I really like Mr. and Mrs. Semple. They are the owners[4] of the farm.

Tonight we had ham, eggs, biscuits[5], honey, jelly[6]-cake, pie, pickles[7], cheese, and tea. We all talked so much.

It's 8:30 p.m. now. I can't wait to go and explore[8] tomorrow.

Good night,
Judy

1. **on a farm** 在農場上
2. **instead of**
   不是⋯⋯而是⋯⋯
3. **heavenly** [`hevənli] (a.)
   天堂般的；十分美好的
4. **owner** [`ounər] (n.)
   擁有者；主人
5. **biscuit** [`bɪskɪt] (n.) 餅乾
6. **jelly** [`dʒeli] (n.)
   果凍；果醬
7. **pickle** [`pɪkəl] (n.)
   醃物（尤指醃黃瓜）
8. **explore** [ɪk`splɔːr] (v.)
   探索；探究

17

July 12th

Dear Daddy-Long-Legs,

How does your secretary know about Lock Willow? It's very strange because Mr. Jervis Pendleton used to[1] own the farm. What a coincidence[2]!

Then he gave the farm to Mrs. Semple who was once[3] his nurse. She often talks about how sweet "Master Jervie" used to be.

1. **used to** 以前曾經
2. **coincidence** [koʊˋɪnsɪdəns] (n.) 巧合
3. **once** [wʌns] (adv.) 曾經
4. **fall off** 從……摔落 (fall-fell-fallen)
5. **beam** [biːm] (n.) 樑木
6. **calf** [kæf] (n.) 犢；小牛
7. **name** [neɪm] (v.) 取名
8. **would love to** 樂於
9. **doughnut** [ˋdoʊnʌt] (n.) 甜甜圈

It is my job to collect the eggs. Yesterday, I fell off[4] a beam[5] trying to collect the eggs.

There are so many chickens, pigs and turkeys here. There are five calves[6] that I have named[7] Sylvia, Sallie, Julia, Judy and Daddy-Long-Legs. I hope you don't mind. Daddy-Long-Legs looks like this:

I would love to[8] send you some doughnuts[9] that I have made.

Yours always,
Judy

18

September 25th

Dear Daddy-Long-Legs,

I am finally a sophomore[1]. I returned[2] last Friday. I was very sad to leave Lock Willow. But it is good to return to something familiar[3].

Some changes have taken place[4]. I'm rooming with[5] Sallie and Julia. We each have our own little rooms and we share a study[6].

1. **sophomore** [ˋsɑːfəmɔːr] (n.) 〔美〕四年制大學二年級生
2. **return** [rɪˋtɜːrn] (v.) 返回
3. **familiar** [fəˋmɪliər] (a.) 熟悉的
4. **take place** 發生
5. **to room with** *sb* 與某人同室友
6. **study** [stʌdi] (n.) 書房
7. **run for** 競選
8. **class president** 班長
9. **chemistry** [ˋkemɪstri] (n.) 化學
10. **unusual** [ʌnˋjuːʒəl] (a.) 不尋常的;異於平常的
11. **subject** [ˋsʌbdʒekt] (n.) 科目
12. **thanks to** 感謝
13. **affectionate** [əˋfekʃənət] (a.) 充滿愛意的

This year, Sallie is running for[7] class president[8]. I think that she is going to win.

I've also started studying chemistry[9]. I still don't know much about it. It's the most unusual[10] subject[11].

I'm learning so much, Daddy, and it's all thanks to[12] you.

Your affectionate[13] orphan,
J. Abbott

A True or False.

T F **1** Judy spent the afternoon with Mr. Pendleton because Julia didn't want to.

T F **2** Judy really enjoyed her time with Mr. Pendleton.

T F **3** Mr. Pendleton was exactly like the other Pendletons.

T F **4** Judy really liked spending her vacation on a farm.

B Write down the sentences according to the example above.

> Mr. Jervis Pendleton owned the farm.
>
> + He does not own the farm anymore.
>
> ⇨ *Mr. Jervis Pendleton used to own the farm.*

1 I played the piano every day.

    + I don't play the piano anymore.

    ⇨ _____

2 There was a tall tree here.

    + Now, there is a tall building instead of the tree.

    ⇨ _____

C Choose the best answer to each question.

❶ Why was Julia angry with Judy?

(a) Because Judy said some bad things about her.

(b) Because Judy spent all the afternoon with her uncle.

(c) Because Judy grew up in an orphanage.

❷ What did Jerusha have to do on the farm?

(a) She had to collect the eggs.

(b) She had to milk the cows.

(c) She had to cook the dinner.

D Fill in the blanks with the given words.

nurse	secretary	coincidence	beam

How does your ❶ _____ know about Lock Willow? It's very strange because Mr. Jervis Pendleton used to own the farm. What a ❷ _____!
Then he gave the farm to Mrs. Semple who was once his ❸ _____. She often talks about how sweet "Master Jervie" used to be. It is my job to collect the eggs. Yesterday, I fell off a ❹ _____ trying to collect the eggs.

· Chapter Four ·

🎧 19 # Independent[1] Judy

March 24th

Dear Daddy-Long-Legs,

So many good things have happened to[2] me. I am sure that I don't deserve[3] everything I have. I have great news! I won the short story[4] contest[5] that the Monthly holds[6] every year.

1. **independent**
   [ˌɪndɪˈpendənt] (a.)
   獨立的;自主的
2. *sth* **happen to** *sb*
   某人發生某事
3. **deserve** [dɪˈzɜːrv] (v.) 應得
4. **short story** 短篇小說
5. **contest** [ˈkɑːntest] (n.) 比賽
6. **hold** [hould] (v.) 舉行
   (hold-held-held)
7. **prize** [praɪz] (n.)
   獎品;獎金
8. **senior** [ˈsiːnjər] (n.)
   大學四年級生
9. **after all** 畢竟;終究

There is a twenty-five dollar prize[7], and it's mine. I still can't believe it.

What is even more special is that usually the winners are seniors[8]. But I am only a sophomore. Maybe I will become a successful author after all[9].

One Point Lesson

◆ **What** is even more special is that usually the winners are seniors. 更特別的是，通常得獎者都是四年級生。

what：在此處作關係代名詞，等於 the thing that。原句可替換為→ The thing that is even more special is that . . . 或更簡單的→ The even more special thing is that . . .

This is **what** I want to buy.
這正是我想要買的（東西）。

I have some other great news, too. Next Friday, Julia, Sallie and I are going to New York. We are going to stay in a hotel and go shopping[1].

On Saturday, we are going to see *Hamlet* at the theater[2] with "Master Jervie." I am so excited about it that I can hardly[3] sleep.

It will be the first time I have stayed in a hotel or gone to the theater. My head is spinning[4] from the excitement.

I'm really looking forward to[5] seeing the play[6]. Especially because we've been studying it in class and I know all of the lines[7].

Yours ever,
Judy

1. **go shopping** 購物；血拼
2. **theater** [ˋθiːətər] (n.) 戲院；劇院
3. **hardly** [ˋhɑːrdli] (adv.) 幾乎不……
4. **spin** [spɪn] (v.) 暈眩 (spin-spun-spun)
5. **look forward to + Ving** 期待……
6. **play** [pleɪ] (n.) 戲劇；舞台劇
7. **lines** [laɪnz] (n.) 台詞

I'm really **looking forward to seeing** the play.
我由衷期待去看這齣戲。

look forward to + V-ing：期待……
can't help + V-ing：不得不……
feel like + V-ing：想要……

I'm **looking forward to meeting** you. 我很期待見到你。
I **can't help thinking** of you. 我不自禁地想你。
I **feel like eating** pizza. 我想吃披薩。

61

April 7th

Dear Daddy-Long-Legs,

I am here in New York! I am amazed at everything I see. Everything is so wonderful but so confusing¹ at the same time².

1. **confusing** [kənˋfjuːzɪŋ] (a.) 令人困惑、迷惑的
2. **at the same time** 同時
3. **describe** [dɪˋskraɪb] (v.) 描述；描寫
4. **try on** 試穿；試戴
5. **in the end** 到最後；末了
6. **loveliest** (a.) 最可愛的（lovely 的最高級）
7. **cost** [kɑːst] (v.) 花費 (cost-cost-cost)

I can't describe[3] everything to you, but I guess you already know. You live here in New York anyway.

Julia and I went shopping today. I saw the most gorgeous hats and Julia tried on[4] so many of them. In the end[5] she bought the loveliest[6] two. I think it is amazing that she can buy any hat she wants without worrying about how much it costs[7].

One Point Lesson

◆ I am **amazed** at everything I see.
我所見到的每一件事物，都令我感到驚異。

amazed：感到驚異的、驚愕的
amazing：令人驚異的、驚愕的
amazed 以主動表示「人」感到驚異；amazing 則以主動表示「物」使人感到驚異。使用時要注意兩者的不同。

e.g. I am **surprised** at the news.
這消息（或新聞）讓我感到意外。
I am **disappointed** with the result.
這結果令我失望。

22

We also met Master Jervie on Saturday afternoon. He took us to[1] a very nice restaurant.

I ordered[2] fish, but I didn't know which fork to use. I accidentally[3] used the wrong one, but the waiter was very kind. He gave me another one.

1. **take** *A* **to** *B* 帶 A 去 B 處
2. **order** [`ɔːrdər] (v.) 點餐
3. **accidentally** [ˌæksə`dentli] (adv.) 不小心地；不經意地

After we ate our meal[4], we went to the theater. It was truly[5] amazing. I still remember every detail[6]. The actors and actresses[7] were marvelous[8].

Oh! One more thing! Master Jervie gave us each a beautiful bunch[9] of flowers. There were lilies of the valley[10] and violets[11].

Isn't he the kindest man? I'm starting to like men more and more because of him.

Yours with love,
Judy

4. **meal** [mi:l] (n.) 餐
5. **truly** [`tru:li] (adv.)
   著實地；的的確確地
6. **detail** [`di:teɪl] (n.)
   細節；細部
7. **actors and actresses**
   男女演員

8. **marvelous** [`mɑ:rvələs] (a.)
   不可思議的；出色的；很棒的
9. **bunch** [bʌntʃ] (n.)
   束（尤指花束）
10. **lily of the valley** 鈴蘭
11. **violet** [`vaɪələt] (n.) 紫羅蘭

23

May 4th

Dear Daddy-Long-Legs,

We had a sports day[1] last Saturday.
It started out with[2] a very cheerful[3] parade[4].
But Sallie and I weren't in the parade. We were
waiting to take part in[5] our events[6].

And guess what?[7] We both won! Sallie won
the pole-vaulting[8] event and I won the fifty-
yard sprint[9] (eight seconds).

Judy Wins the
Fifty-Yard Sprint

1. **sports day** 運動日
2. **start out with**
   以……開始
3. **cheerful** [`tʃɪrfəl] (a.)
   充滿歡樂的；歡欣鼓舞的
4. **parade** [pə`reɪd] (n.) 遊行
5. **take part in** 參加
6. **event** [ɪ`vɛnt] (n.) 運動項目
7. **Guess what?** 猜怎麼著？
8. **pole-vaulting** [poʊl vɔːltɪŋ]
   (n.) 撐竿跳
9. **sprint** [sprɪnt] (n.) 短跑
10. **at the end of the day**
    一天結束之際

It was all very exciting and we felt so good at the end of the day[10]. Everyone was very tired and so we all went to bed very early that night.

I love you always,
Judy

24

June 4th

Dear Daddy,

I have been very busy these days[1] studying for my examinations. They begin tomorrow.

The weather here is so beautiful that it is very difficult to stay inside.[2] But I must continue to[3] study hard.

1. **these days**
   這些日子；近來
2. **inside** [ɪnˋsaɪd] (adv.) 室內
3. **continue to** 繼續
4. **once** [wʌns] (conj.) 一旦
5. **plan to** 打算
6. **seaside** [ˋsiːsaɪd] (n.) 海邊
7. **tutor** [ˋtjuːtər] (v.) 當家教
8. **earn** [ɜːrn] (v.) 賺取
9. **object** [əbˋdʒekt] (v.)
   反對；反駁

Once⁴ the examinations are finished, our vacation will be here. I can't wait. Can you guess what I am planning to⁵ do this vacation?

Lock Willow? Sallie and her family? No, I am going to the seaside⁶ to tutor⁷ a girl and her younger sister. I will teach them English and Latin. Each month, I will be earning⁸ fifty dollars!

Please don't object⁹ to my plan. I am becoming very independent thanks to you.

I hope that you have a wonderful summer, Daddy.

Yours always,
Judy

One Point Lesson

I **have been** very busy these days studying for my examinations. 為了考試，這些日子我好忙，一直在讀書。

此句為完成進行式，表示已經開始的動作仍在進行中。

I **have been** here for a week.
我到這兒已有一個星期了。

June 10th

Dear Daddy,

This is a very difficult letter for me to write to you.

You have given me a wonderful opportunity[1]. But I feel that it is my responsibility to start supporting[2] myself this summer instead of you sending me to Europe.

I feel very strongly[3] about this. It is so kind of you to offer me such an opportunity though[4].

1. **opportunity** [ˌɑ:pərˋtu:nəti] (n.) 機會
2. **support** [səˋpɔːrt] (v.) 供養
3. **strongly** [ˋstrɔːŋli] (adv.) 強烈地
4. **though** [ðou] (adv.) 不過
5. **be about to** 即將
6. **post** [poust] (v.) 郵寄
7. **force** *sb* **to do** *sth* 強迫某人做某事
8. **refuse** [rɪˋfjuːz] (v.) 拒絕
9. **make one's decision** 作自己的決定
10. **independently** [ˌɪndɪˋpendəntli] (adv.) 獨立地；自主地
11. **repay** [rɪˋpeɪ] (v.) 回報；償還

Four days later

I was about to[5] post[6] this letter to you when I met Master Jervie. He has invited me to Europe as well.

He said it was an important part of my education. I almost said yes. But one thing stopped me.

He was almost trying to force[7] me to go. I refuse[8] to be forced to do anything. I want to make my own decisions[9] independently[10].

To repay[11] you for your kindness, I will become a wise and independent woman.

Yours ever,
Judy

One Point Lesson

◆ **It is so kind of you to offer** me such an opportunity though.
不過，您給我這樣的一個機會，真是好心。

It is+ *adj.* **+ of + ** *sb* **+ to do** *sth*
某人做某事，是……的

e.g. **It is** very **nice of you to help** the poor.
你幫助窮困者，真是仁厚之舉。

A Match the two parts to make reasonable sentences.

1 I have been very busy these days •

2 I saw the most gorgeous hats, •

3 I accidentally used the wrong fork •

4 I feel that it is my responsibility •

5 After we ate our meal, •

• **a** to start supporting myself.

• **b** studying for my examinations.

• **c** and Julia tried on so many of them.

• **d** we went to the theater.

• **e** but the waiter was very kind.

B True or False.

T F ❶ Judy won the short story contest.

T F ❷ Judy went to New York alone.

T F ❸ Judy had never seen a play before.

T F ❹ Judy bought some hats without worrying how much they cost.

T F ❺ Judy was going to spend her vacation at Lock Willow.

C Correct the mistakes.

I was about ❶ posting this letter to you when I met Master Jervie. He ❷ has invite me to Europe as well. He said it was an important part of my education.
I almost said yes. But one thing stopped me. He was almost trying to force me to go. I refuse to ❸ to force to do anything.

❶ _____ ❷ _____ ❸ _____

Before You Read

write a letter
寫信

send a letter
寄信

recieve/get a letter
收到一封信

mail 郵件	**envelope** 信封	**stamp** 郵票	**address** 地址	**postcard** 明信片
post box 信箱；郵筒	**post office** 郵局	**zip code** 郵遞區號	**mail carrier** 郵差	**e-mail** 電子郵件

How to Write an English Letter

① Address 地址
② Date 日期
③ Inside address 信文內地址
④ Salutation 稱謂
⑤ Body 正文
⑥ Complimentary closing 結尾問候語
⑦ Signature 署名
⑧ Postscript 附註

① 215 Fergussen Hall

② June 9th

③ 244 Oak Street New York

④ Dear Daddy-Long-Legs,

⑤ Happy day! I've just finished my last examination—physiology. And now I'm looking forward to enjoying summer vacation! I'm going to read a lot of books this summer.

This letter will be a short one because I have to pack for the holidays on the Lock Willow farm.

I'll write in detail as soon as possible!

⑥ Yours ever,
⑦ *Judy*

⑧ P.S. Here is my physiology exam.
Do you think you could have passed?

· Chapter Five ·

🎧 26 # The Surprising[1] Truth

June 19th

Dear Daddy-Long-Legs,

Can you believe this? I can't. I have finally finished college and received my degree.

Thank you so much for the roses that you sent me. I carried them in the graduation[2] procession[3].

1. **surprising** [sə`praızıŋ] (a.)
令人意外的；驚喜的
2. **graduation** [ˌgradʒu`eıʃən]
(n.) 畢業；畢業生（集合詞）；
畢業典禮
3. **procession** [prə`seʃən] (n.)
行列；隊伍的行進
4. **do nothing but**
什麼都沒做；除了
5. **Bachelor of Arts** 文學士

Now I am at Lock Willow doing nothing but[4] writing my book. Master Jervie is coming to Lock Willow sometime in August. I wish you would come, but I know that will never happen.

Judy Abbott,
Bachelor of Arts[5]

July 24th

Dearest Daddy-Long-Legs,

I have had such a wonderful summer. I have been writing as much as possible[1]. I just wish that each day were longer. Then, I could write even[2] more.

This is going to be a real book, Daddy. I'm so excited about this one.

I have such a wonderful place to work here at Lock Willow. I have the best scenery[3] in the world, lots of food, a wonderful bed and all the paper and ink I need.

I think I'm the luckiest girl in the world.

Still wishing I could meet you,
Judy

1. **as . . . as possible**
   盡可能……
2. **even** [`i:vən] (adv.)
   更加；更
3. **scenery** [`si:nəri] (n.)
   風景；景色
4. **advice** [əd`vaɪs] (n.)
   忠告；意見；指點

September 19th

Dear Daddy,

I need your advice[4] on quite a serious topic[5]. I would rather[6] see you to talk to you about it.

I'm worried that your secretary will read this letter, and I want to keep it private[7]. Please let me come and see you. I am very unhappy right now[8].

Judy

5. **topic** [ˈtɑːpɪk] (n.)
   話題；題目
6. **would rather** 寧可

7. **keep in private**
   保密（private：私密的）
8. **right now** 此時此刻

October 3rd

Dear Daddy-Long-Legs,

I just received your message[1]. I am so sorry to hear that you have been ill[2]. I wish I had known before I bothered you with my problem.

I will tell you my problem in this letter but please burn[3] it after you read it. However, before I tell you, I'm sending you a check[4] for one thousand dollars. I sold my book.

1. **message** [`mesɪdʒ] (n.) 訊息；消息
2. **ill** [ɪl] (a.) 生病的
3. **burn** [bɜːrn] (v.) 燒
4. **check** [tʃek] (n.) 支票
5. *sth* **means a lot to** *sb* 某事對某人來說意義重大
6. **owe** [oʊ] (v.) 欠
7. **be able to** 能夠
8. **affection** [ə`fekʃən] (n.) 深情；摯愛；感情
9. **gratitude** [`grætɪtuːd] (n.) 感激
10. **token** [`toʊkən] (n.) 表示；象徵
11. **appreciative** [ə`priːʃətɪv] (a.) 感激的；銘感的
12. **care for** 關愛；在乎

It will really mean a lot to me[5] if you take this check. I already owe[6] you so much which I will only ever be able to[7] repay with my affection[8] and gratitude[9]. This is just a small token[10] of how appreciative[11] of you I am.

Here is my problem. You know that I have always cared very deeply for[12] you, but now there is another man who I care for even more. He is Master Jervie.

One Point Lesson

I wish I had known before I bothered you with my problem.
但願我拿我的問題煩擾您之前，已經知道此事了。

I wish + 代名詞 + had + 過去分詞：
當 wish 是用來表示對現在不可能實現的願望時，子句中要用假設法的過去式。又因子句是要表示已經做過某事或有過某種經驗，所以用過去完成式。

e.g **I wish I had bought the book.**
但願我（已經）買了那本書。

I know you don't know him, but I wish you did. He is so kind and generous, and we get on[1] extremely well together.

We always laugh about the same things. When I am not with him, I miss him more than anything else in the world.

Have you ever loved anyone? Unless[2] you have, you can't know how I feel.

I truly care for him, but I have refused to marry[3] him. I couldn't tell him I am an orphan. And I feel that someone like me has no right[4] to marry into a family like his.

If he married me, he would regret[5] it. I could never explain my reasons[6] to him.

1. **get on** 相處
2. **unless** [ʌn`lɛs] (conj.) 除非
3. **marry** [`mæri] (v.) 嫁
4. **right** [raɪt] (n.) 權利;資格
5. **regret** [rɪ`grɛt] (v.) 後悔;悔憾
6. **explain the reason** 說明原因
7. **heartbroken** [`hɑrt͵breɪkən] 心碎的
8. **ever since** 從此以後
9. **pneumonia** [nu:`moʊnjə] (n.) 肺炎
10. **confused** [kən`fju:zd] (a.) 迷惘的;困惑的

That was about two months ago. I've been heartbroken[7] ever since[8] then. I haven't heard from him at all. But Julia told me that he was very sick with pneumonia[9]. I guess he is very unhappy. What do you think I should do?

A very confused[10] Judy

30

October 6th

Dearest Daddy-Long-Legs,

I'm excited to finally have the chance to[1] meet you. Half past four next Wednesday afternoon! I won't forget.

I've been in New York three times now so I'll be able to find the way. I can't believe that I'm going to meet you.

I've thought about you for such a long time[2] that you seem hardly real. Thank you for letting me visit you when you are not that well.

Affectionately[3],
Jerusha

1. **have the chance to**
   有⋯⋯的機會
2. **for such a long time**
   這麼久的時間

3. **affectionately**
   [əˋfekʃənətli] (adv.)
   情深地
4. **get better** 好轉；變好

Thursday Morning

My Very Dearest Master-Jervie-Daddy-Long-
Legs-Pendleton-Smith,

I can hardly sleep these days because I am
so happy and excited. Yet, I feel terrible that
you have been so sick. Please get better[4] really
fast.

I'm worried that I only dreamed what
happened yesterday. We only had thirty
minutes together, but I will remember every
detail.

One Point Lesson

● **Half past four next Wednesday afternoon!**
   下週三下午四點半！

英文中對時刻的說法至少有三種，以 4 點 30 分來說，可說
成：① four thirty ② half past four ③ thirty to five

e.g. 4:00 = four o'clock   3:50 = ten to four
     4:15 = a quarter past four   3:45 = a quarter to four

31

I am a very different girl now compared to[1] the girl who left Lock Willow yesterday morning.

I got up early yesterday, ate breakfast by candlelight[2] and took the train to New York.

The whole time I was singing to myself, "You're going to see Daddy-Long-Legs."

I came to your house but I was almost too[3] afraid to go in. Your butler[4] was very kind to me when I entered your home. I waited excitedly in the drawing room[5]. Then, your butler showed me into your room.

1. **compare to** 相較於……
2. **candlelight** [ˋkændlaɪt] (n.) 燭光
3. **too . . . to . . .** 太……而不能……
4. **butler** [ˋbʌtlər] (n.) 大宅中的內務總管
5. **drawing room** 會客室
6. **fireplace** [ˋfaɪrpleɪs] (n.) 壁爐

It was quite dark, so I couldn't see very well at first. I first noticed the fire in the fireplace[6]. I looked over[7] and saw a large chair. A man was sitting there with lots of pillows[8] and blankets[9]. I looked more closely[10] and realized[11] it was you.

7. **look over** 看過去
8. **pillow** [`pɪlou] (n.) 枕頭；靠墊
9. **blanket** [`blæŋkɪt] (n.) 毯子
10. **closely** [`klousli] (adv.) 仔細地
11. **realize** [`rɪəlaɪz] (v.) 發覺；恍悟

32

I thought that it was a joke[1] that Daddy was playing.

You started laughing at that moment[2] and asked, "My dear Judy, didn't you guess that I was Daddy-Long-Legs?"

I couldn't say anything at that moment. So many things went through my mind. I thought of so many clues[3] that could have told me that Daddy was you.

What shall I call you now? Daddy? Jervis? Jervie? Please let me know.

Our thirty minutes together passed by[4] too quickly. I wanted to stay longer, but your doctor wouldn't let me.

1. **joke** [dʒouk] (n.) 玩笑
   （play a joke，開玩笑）
2. **at that moment**
   在那一刻；當時
3. **clue** [kluː] (n.) 線索；暗示
4. **pass by** 過去；逝去
5. **trip** [trɪp] (n.) 旅行
6. **daze** [deɪz] (n.)
   暈眩、惶惑或恍惚的狀態
7. **belong to** 屬於
8. **do one's best** 盡一己之力
9. **love letter** 情書

My trip[5] back to Lock Willow was a strange one. I was in a daze[6] the whole way. But I am so happy.

I miss you so much, but I know we will be together soon. We belong to[7] each other now. I feel so happy that I finally belong to someone. I will always do my best[8] to make you happy.

I am yours forever,
Judy

P.S. I have never written a love letter[9] before but isn't it strange that I know how?

A Match the two parts according to meanings.

1 graduation •　　• a very bad or important

2 serious •　　• b a piece of cloth used to keep warm

3 heartbroken •　　• c thankfulness

4 gratitude •　　• d a ceremony to finish college

5 bother •　　• e extremely sad

6 blanket •　　• f to trouble or annoy

B Fill in the blanks with the given words.

when	so	unless	if

1 It will mean a lot to me _____ you take this check.

2 _____ you have ever loved someone, you can't know how I feel.

3 It was quite dark _____ I couldn't see very well.

4 _____ I am not with him, I miss him more than anything else in the world.

C Rearrange the following sentences in chronological order.

1 Judy finally realized Master Jervie was her "Daddy."

2 Judy wrote her problem in the letter to Daddy-Long-Legs.

3 Judy left Lock Willow and headed for New York.

4 Judy entered Daddy-Long-Legs' room.

5 Judy wrote a letter after knowing the whole truth.

D Fill in the blanks with the given words.

wish   deeply   another   problem

Here is my **1** _____. You know that I have always cared very **2** _____ for you, but now there is **3** _____ man who I care even more for. He is Master Jervie. I know that you don't know him but I **4** _____ you did.

Appendixes

1 Basic Grammar

要增強英文閱讀理解能力，應練習找出英文的主結構。
要擁有良好的英語閱讀能力，首先要理解英文的段落結構。

「英文的閱讀理解從「分解文章」開始」

英文的文章是以「有意義的詞組」（指帶有意義的語句）所構成的。用（／）符號來區別各個意義語塊，請試著掌握其中的意義。

主詞 ◯ 動詞

某樣東西　如何做
（人、事、物）

He runs (very fast).
他　跑　（非常快）

It is raining .
雨　正在下

主詞 ◯ 動詞 ◯ 補語 （補充的話）

某樣東西　　如何做　　怎麼樣
（人、事、物）

This is a cat .
這　是　一隻貓。

The cat is very big .
那隻貓　是　非常　大

主詞 → 動詞 → 受詞

某樣東西　　如何做　　什麼
（人、事、物）

人，事物，兩者皆是受詞

| I | like | you | . |

我　喜歡　你。

| You | gave | me | some flowers | . |

你　給　我　　一些花

主詞 → 動詞 → 受詞 → 補語

某樣東西　　如何做　　什麼　　怎麼樣／什麼
（人、事、物）

| You | make | me | happy | . |

你　使（讓）我　幸福（快樂）

| I | saw | him | running | . |

我　看到　他　　跑

　　其他修飾語或副詞等，都可以視為為了完成句子而臨時、額外、特別附加的，閱讀起來便可更加輕鬆；先具備這些基本概念，再閱讀部分精選篇章，最後做了解文章整體架構的練習。

On the first Wednesday of every month,

（在）每個月的第一個星期三，

| the trustees | of the John Grier Orphanage | came | to visit. |

董事們　　約翰·格利爾孤兒院的　　來　訪視

| Jerusha Abbott | hated | these days | the most. |

茉露莎·亞伯特　討厭　這些日子　最

| She | was | the oldest orphan | in the home. |

她　是　年紀最大的孤兒　在孤兒院內

She   had   the responsibility
她   有   責任

to make sure everything was completely clean.
　務　必使　一切　　　一塵不染

She also had to clean every one of the ninety-seven orphans.
她　還　必須　弄乾淨　　九十七名孤兒中的每一個

Today was one of those days .
今天　　是　　一個這種日子

Now the day was over and she was sitting down ,
現在　　這天　是　結束了　而　她　　正坐下來，

thinking about the day.
　回想著這一天。

She was dreaming of driving away in a similar car
她　　正夢想著　　　開著同樣的汽車離去，

when she heard a familiar voice.
　這時聽到一個熟悉的聲音。

"Jerusha! You have to go to the office now!"
「茉露莎！ 妳　必須　去　辦公室 立刻！」

However, at the meeting today, you were discussed .
　「不過　在今天的會議中，　妳　　被討論到

Now you are too old to stay at the orphanage.
現在　妳　是　年紀太大　（不適合）待在孤兒院。

Normally, you would be expected to work ,
正常情況下，妳　會　　　被期待　去工作，

but considering your excellent grades, especially in English,
但是　　考慮到妳優異的學業成績，尤其是英文方面，

this gentleman has offered to send you to college".
這位紳士 已表示 要送妳 上大學。」

Jerusha was stunned . "To college!" she said .
茱露莎 是 呆若木雞。「上大學！」 她 說。

"Yes, this gentleman thinks you have great talent
「是的， 這位紳士 認為 妳很有天賦，

and wants you to become a writer .
而 想要 妳 成為一名作家。

He will pay your board and tuition for four years.
他 會 支付 妳的食宿和學費 四年。

He will also give you an allowance of thirty-five dollars a month.
他 還會 給 妳 一筆零用金 每個月三十五元。

In return, you must write a letter every month
作為回報，妳 必須 寫 一 信 每個月

telling him of your progress.
告訴他妳的進展。

The letters will be written to Mr. John Smith.
信 要 被寫 給給約翰‧史密斯先生

It is not his real name .
它 是 不 他的真實姓名。

He will not write back to you, so don't ask him any questions .
他 不會 回信 給妳，所以 別問 他 任何問題。

You must always remember to have a respectful tone ".
妳 必須 時時 記得 要有一種尊敬的口氣。」

Jerusha didn't know what to say .
茱露莎 不知道 要說什麼。

She was full of excitement.
她 是 充滿 興奮。

Guide to Listening Comprehension

 When listening to the story, use some of the techniques shown below. If you take time to study some phonetic characteristics of English, listening will be easier.

Get in the flow of English.

English creates a rhythm formed by combinations of strong and weak stress intonations. Each word has its particular stress that combines with other words to form the overall pattern of stress or rhythm in a particular sentence.

When you are speaking and listening to English, it is essential to get in the flow of the rhythm of English. It takes a lot of practice to get used to such a rhythm. So, you need to start by identifying the stressed syllable in a word.

Listen for the strongly stressed words and phrases.

In English, key words and phrases that are essential to the meaning of a sentence are stressed louder. Therefore, pay attention to the words stressed with a higher pitch. When listening to an English recording for the first time, what matters most is to listen for a general understanding of what you hear. Do not to try to hear every single word. Most of the unstressed words are articles or auxiliary verbs, which don't play an important role in the general context. At this level, you can ignore them.

Pay attention to liaisons.

In reading English, words are written with a space between them. There isn't such an obvious guide when it comes to listening to English. In oral English, there are many cases when the sounds of words are linked with adjacent words.

For instance, let's think about the phrase "**take off**," which can be used in "take off your clothes." "Take off your clothes" doesn't sound like [teɪk ɔːf] with each of the words completely and clearly separated from the others. Instead, it sounds as if almost all the words in context are slurred together, [ˈteɪkɔːf], for a more natural sound.

Shadow the voice of the native speaker.

Finally, you need to mimic the voice of the native speaker. Once you are sure you know how to pronounce all the words in a sentence, try to repeat them like an echo. Listen to the book again, but this time you should try a fun exercise while listening to the English.

This exercise is called "shadowing." The word "shadow" means a dark shade that is formed on a surface. When used as a verb, the word refers to the action of following someone or something like a shadow. In this exercise, pretend you are a parrot and try to shadow the voice of the native speaker.

Try to mimic the reader's voice by speaking at the same speed, with the same strong and weak stresses on words, and pausing or stopping at the same points.

Experts have already proven this technique to be effective. If you practice this shadowing exercise, your English speaking and listening skills will improve by leaps and bounds. While shadowing the native speaker, don't forget to pay attention to the meaning of each phrase and sentence.

Listen to what you want to shadow many times. Start out by just trying to shadow a few words or a sentence.

 Mimic the CD out loud. You can shadow everything the speaker says as if you are singing a round, or you also can speak simultaneously with the recorded voice of the native speaker.

 As you practice more, try to shadow more. For instance, shadow a whole sentence or paragraph instead of just a few words.

Chapter One page 14 🎧 33

On the (**❶**) (   ) of every month, the trustees of the John Grier Orphanage came to visit. Jerusha Abbott (**❷**) these days the most. She was the oldest orphan in the home. She had the (**❸**) to make sure everything was (**❹**) clean.

❶ first Wednesday：first 這個字，由於最後兩個字母 st 都是吐氣音，讀音很輕，尤其如果後續的字的重音在第一音節時，st 常常聽不出來。自己口說時也記得不要唸得太用力。Wednesday 這個字，要注意第一個 d 和第二個 e 不發音，s 讀音為 /z/。

❷ hated：這個字要注意 ted 的發音 /tɪd/。e 是短音，t 是吐氣音，所以聽或說時，都要注意它的發音很輕。字尾 d 雖是有聲音，但因為在字尾，聽或說時常會連著下一個字，所以發音是含在嘴裡的。

❸ responsibility：這個字有六個音節，因此要特別注意重音。通常超過四個音節的字，都有雙重音，一主一副。這個字的主重音在 bi，副重音在 pon。同時在主重音前的 si 發音很輕，且 i 字唸得快時幾乎不發音。

❹ completely：這個字只有三個音節，重音在 le，且這個 e 發長母音。而 te 的 e 不發音，因此 tely 讀音是相連的雙子音，這時吐氣音的 t 就得退居幕後，由 l 在台前發聲。

以下為《長腿叔叔》各章節的前半部。一開始若能聽清楚發音，之後就沒有聽力的負擔。先聽過摘錄的章節，之後再反覆聆聽括弧內單字的發音，並仔細閱讀各種發音的説明。以下都是以英語的典型發音為基礎，所做的簡易説明，即使這裡未提到的發音，也可以配合音檔反覆聆聽，如此一來聽力必能更上層樓。

Chapter Two page 28 🎧 34

I am so happy to be here. I love you for sending me here. It is (❶) (　　) place. My room is high in a tower. There are two girls here(❷) (　). One is Sallie McBride who has red hair and a turned-up nose. The other is Julia Rutledge Pendleton. She comes from (❸) (　) (　) wealthiest families in New York.

❶ **an amazing**：an 這個字與 a 這個字讀音時所受的待遇不同。當強調「一個」時，a 偶爾可以喧賓奪主，但是 an 則沒有這種機會。就像 an amazing (place)，兩字連著唸時，主角必是 amazing。不過，amazing 的字首 a 發音很輕，讓 an 有完全被聽到的機會。

❷ **with me**：with 這個字要注意它的 th。有時是夾在齒間的有聲音，有時是藏在齒內的無聲音。當後續字的字首是子音，例如 with me，則 th 常是無聲音，若後續字的字首是母音，例如 with you，則 th 常是有聲音。

❸ **one of the**：三個字連著唸時，幾乎成一個字，而重音在 one。of 要注意，它的 o 是唸作 /ə/，f 是唸作 /v/，不要唸成 /əf/。the 要注意 e 是發聲的。不過三字相連時，因為 of 和 the 都只有一個音節，且都是短母音，所以唸起來務必要做配角，甚至半隱形。

This (❶) (　　) gorgeous in May. Everything is in bloom. Everyone is outside enjoying the fine weather. We have (❷) (　　), but no one is thinking about them. Vacation will be here soon! I am so happy, too! I am going to work hard this summer and (❸) (　　) great author.

❶ **campus is**：要先注意 is 這個字。is 輕讀時只發 /s/ 或 /z/: 這時當 is 是跟在「s, sh, ch」這幾個無聲子音後面時，讀作 /z/。因此，campus Is 連著唸而不重讀 is 時，campus 的 s 退讓，幾乎只聽得到 is 的 /z/ 音。is 重讀時才發音為 /iz/ 或 /ɪz/。而在此處，由於全句的重心在 is 的下一個字，gorgeous，故而 is 是輕讀。

❷ **examinations soon**：先看 examinations。此字有五個音節，主重音在 na，副重音在 xa，因此這個字不易輕讀。但是，examinations 與 soon 連讀時，音調重心在 soon，因此要盡可能輕讀 examinations。此外，由於此字字尾加了複數 s，且 soon 是長母音，因此與 soon 連讀時，複數 s 幾乎聽不出來。

❸ **become a**：become 這個字的重音在第二音節 com，e 不發音。而當 a 是跟在前一個字的重音節後面，無論該重音節中的母音是否為長母音，a 都作輕讀，讀音是 /ə/。a 作重讀時，讀音才是 /ei/，而通常重讀都是為了強調語氣。

So many good things have (**❶**) (　) me. I am sure that I don't deserve everything I have. I have (**❷**) (　)! I won the (**❸**) (　) contest that the Monthly holds every year.

❶ happened to：happened 與 hated 不同之處，在字尾的 -ed。前者只發 /d/。不過兩者相同處在於後面連接 to 時，由於 d 和 t 發音近似，字尾 d 要讓位給後接母音的 to。也就是唸得快時，字尾 d 幾乎不發音。但是，聽或説的人要有發音的意識，或者應該説，要有文法和時態的意識。

❷ great news：當字尾是 p, t, k 等吐氣音時，除非下一個字的字首是相同的吐氣音字母，否則 p 唸作近似 b；t 唸作近似 d；k 唸作近似 g。所以 great news 唸得快時，會近似 gread news。

注意，news 的字尾 s 發音為 /z/。而在美語中，news 的 ew 可唸作 /u/，也可唸作 /ju/。

❸ short story：當字首為雙吐氣音時，如 story，則第二個吐氣音的讀音自然地改為非吐氣音；即 p 唸作 b；t 唸作 d；k 唸作 g。例如 student，唸作 sdudent；story 唸作 sdory。而在 short story 中，前字字尾是 t，後字字首是 s，唸得快時，讀音會近似 shorts dory。

Can you believe this? I (❶). I have finally finished college and received my degree. Thank you so much for the roses that you sent me. I (❷) (   ) in the graduation procession.

❶ **can't**：在美語中，can't 母音與 can 重讀時的母音相同，而它的字尾是 t，發音很輕，所以 can't 這個字，無論是聽或唸它，一定要注意它的重音，否則很容易與 can 混淆。同時要記住，can 這個字一般唸起來都是輕讀，母音發作 /ə/，唯有用來強調語氣時，才會重讀 /æ/。

❷ **carried them**：此二字連讀時，情況與 happened to 類似。carried 字尾是 d，而 them 字首是 th 的有聲音，兩者發音近似，因此字尾要讓位給字首，唸起來幾乎聽不到 d。不過還是要提醒，聽或說的人要有發音的意識，要有文法和時態的意識。

4

Listening Comprehension

38 **A** Listen to the CD and select the correct person who is described in each sentence.

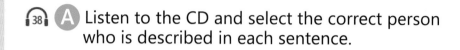

Sallie   Master Jervie   Judy   Julia   Daddy-Long-Legs

1 _____ **2** _____ **3** _____ **4** _____ **5** _____

39 **B** Listen to the CD and fill in the blanks.

1 I am so _____ by everything here.

2 I have _____ my room.

3 In fact, my teacher said that my writing was amazingly _____.

4 I have _____ all over my body.

5 You never answered my question. Are you _____?

6 I'm worried that your _____ will read this letter, and I want to keep it _____.

🎧 40 C Listen to the CD and choose the correct answer.

1 _____?

(a) Because Julia was rich.

(b) Because Julia was very smart.

(c) Because Julia ignored her.

2 _____?

(a) Tall, old and unhappy.

(b) Tall, bald and young.

(c) Tall, old and lively.

3 _____?

(a) Because she didn't want to go to Europe.

(b) Because he tried to force her to go with him.

(c) Because she didn't have enough money to go.

🎧 41 D Listen to the CD and choose the correct answer

1 _____ •   • (a) has no right to marry into a family like his.

2 _____ •   • (b) to hear that you have been ill.

3 _____ •   • (c) studying for my examinations.

Translation

　　美國作家珍‧韋伯斯特（Jean Webster，1876–1916），1876 年生於紐約弗里多尼亞（Fredonia）的富裕人家，受洗時以愛麗絲‧珍‧錢德勒‧韋伯斯特為聖名。

　　因母親那方的關係，她是著名美國作家馬克吐溫（Mark Twain）的親戚。愛麗絲‧韋伯斯特在珍‧葛雷女子寄宿學校上學時的室友是個也叫愛麗絲的女孩，為了避免混淆，她將名字改為珍‧韋伯斯特。1901 年，她以英語文學、經濟學雙主修畢業於瓦薩大學（Vassar College）。

　　她大學時代便為學校雜誌與報紙寫了數篇故事。她對孤兒院改革、監獄改革的關注，也成為小說著作的背景。

　　第一本短篇小說合輯《當貝蒂上大學》（When Patty Went to College）為在校時寫成，1903 年問世後大受歡迎。之後《長腿叔叔》（Daddy-Long-Legs, 1912）與《親愛的敵人》（Dear Enemy, 1915）出版，她成為出名作家。她充滿機智的著作不僅風評甚佳，風格也被稱作美國理想主義（idealism）。

　　珍‧韋伯斯特 1915 年結婚，1916 年女兒出生不久後，她便因難產去世。令人悲傷的是，她的早逝使她錯失機會享受人生與撰寫更多佳作。雖然英年早逝，但今日她的著作今日仍被閱讀，並且持續啟發世上許多女性。

故事介紹　p. 5

　　孤兒茉露莎‧亞伯特（Jerusha Abbott）在約翰‧格利爾孤兒院的日子過得不好。她有寫作天分並滿懷夢想，而現在，一位不具名的富有資助人出現，支持她讀大學，只要求茉露莎每月將大學日常點滴寫信詳述給他。茱露莎將這奇怪但仁慈的男人取名為「長腿叔叔」。

《長腿叔叔》是茱露莎寫給資助人的書信合輯。過去有許多小說以書信體寫成，但這本小說特別在其饒富趣味與觸動人心。小說鮮明勾勒每個角色的獨特性格，尤其顯著刻畫茱露莎的聰明開朗的個性。然而，此書的真諦在於顯露良善、人性與眾生平等的價值。

［第一章］藍色星期三

`p. 14–15` 每個月的第一個星期三，約翰‧格利爾孤兒院的董事們都會前來訪視。茱露莎‧亞伯特最討厭這種日子。她是孤兒院內年紀最大的孤兒，她要負責使一切務必一塵不染，還得把九十七名孤兒統統打理得乾乾淨淨。

今天就是這種日子。現在一天結束了，她正坐下來，回想著這一天。

女院長莉佩特太太讓茱露莎整天忙個不停。茱露莎望向窗外，目視著董事們驅車穿過孤兒院大門。正當她夢想著開著同樣的汽車離去之際，聽到一個熟悉的聲音。

`p. 16–17` 「茱露莎！妳要立刻去辦公室！」是湯米‧迪倫。他也是院內的孤兒。

一股恐慌感貫穿茱露莎的全身。「我做錯什麼了嗎？」她心想。

「是三明治不夠好吃嗎？天呀！還是哪個孤兒對誰魯莽了嗎？」

她走向莉佩特太太的辦公室時，看見一名男子的背影。他在走廊上投下長長的影子。他的雙腿和雙臂都好修長，影子看起來活像腿長長的幽靈蜘蛛。

茱露莎走進辦公室。莉佩特太太立刻開口：「茱露莎！我有消息告訴妳。妳看到剛剛離開的那位紳士了嗎？」

「我只看到他的背影。」茱露莎回答。

p. 18–19 「他是本院最重要的一位董事。他叫我不要向妳透露他的名字。他不想讓妳知道。」

「她幹嘛告訴我這個？」茱露莎心想。

莉佩特太太一逕說道：「妳還記得查爾斯・班頓和亨利・福瑞茲嗎？嗯，這位紳士供他們兩個和其他幾個男生上了大學。在這之前，他只挑選了男生。

他不太喜歡女生。不過呢，在今天的會議中有討論到了妳。妳現在年紀太大了，不適合待在孤兒院。一般來說，妳應該去工作了，但是考量到妳學業成績優異，尤其是英文方面，因此這位紳士已表明要供妳上大學。」

p. 20–21 茱露莎呆若木雞。「上大學！」她說。

「是的，這位紳士認為妳很有天賦，想要妳成為一名作家。他會支付妳大學四年的食宿和學費。他還會給妳一筆零用金，每個月三十五元。妳必須每個月寫一封信，把妳的學習進展告訴他作為回報。

信就寫給約翰・史密斯先生。這不是他的真實姓名。他不會回信給妳，所以別問他任何問題。妳務必時時記得，要用尊敬的口氣。」

茱露莎不知道該說什麼好，她滿心興奮，只說：「是的，謝謝您，院長。」說完，她離開了辦公室。

p. 22–23

佛格森樓 215 室，9 月 24 日

親愛的供孤兒上大學的好心董事：

我終於來到大學這裡了。這裡的一切都教我驚歎。我每次出去仍舊會迷路。過些日子，我會寫給您一封信描述這地方。

我要到星期一才開始上課，可是我想要立刻寫封信給您。

我以前從未寫過什麼信，所以現在寫信感覺似乎很奇怪。

　　昨天早上我動身之前，莉佩特太太告訴我要非常尊敬您，可是既然我不認識您，要怎麼尊敬呢？

p. 24–25 對於您，我只知道三件事：

　　1. 您很高。

　　2. 您很有錢。

　　3. 您討厭女生。

　　我為什麼必須叫您約翰·史密斯先生？如果我叫您親愛的討厭女生先生，或親愛的富翁先生，那就不太有禮貌。

　　不過，若叫您親愛的長腿叔叔如何？您介意嗎？我希望您覺得沒關係，它只是個暱稱，我們別告訴莉佩特太太。

　　晚鐘響了！熄燈！晚安，長腿叔叔。

最尊敬您的，

茱露莎·亞伯特

[第二章] 開始大學生涯

p. 28–29

10 月 1 日

親愛的長腿叔叔：

　　我好高興來到這裡。我愛您因為您讓我來這裡唸書。這是個令人驚歎的地方。

　　我的房間在一座塔樓的高處。有兩個女生跟我住在一起。一個是莎莉·麥布萊德，有一頭紅髮和一個翹鼻子。

　　另一個是茱莉亞·羅莉吉·潘鐸頓，她出身紐約最富裕的一個家庭。

我好高興有自己的房間，以前都得和許多人共用一間。

今天這封信會很短。我希望能成為籃球隊的一員，我知道我個子不高，但是我反應快。我可以比其他女生移動得更快。下一回我再給您寫一封較長的信。

加入籃球隊的事祝我好運吧！

您永遠的，
茱露莎‧亞伯特

p. 30~31

10 月 10 日

親愛的長腿叔叔：

我裝潢了我的房間。我買了一些黃色窗簾、褐色椅墊、一張紅木書桌、一把籐椅和一塊小褐色地毯。現在房間看起來好看多了。

我實在很喜歡我現在生活的地方。我真的很喜歡莎莉‧麥布萊德，但是我不喜歡茱莉亞‧羅莉吉‧潘鐸頓。她從不花心力對我友善。

我現在正研讀許多科目，像幾何、物理、法文、拉丁文，還有英文，這是我最喜歡的科目。事實上，老師說我的上一份英文報告原創性極佳。想想我是在一個不鼓勵原創性的地方長大，老師的這句話不是太棒了嗎？

p. 32~33 我知道，我不該說孤兒院的壞話。您知道，沒有人曉得我是在孤兒院長大的。我不想要跟別的女生不同，不過我告訴了莎莉‧麥布萊德我的父母都不在了。

我告訴她，是一位仁厚的老紳士送我來念大學。唔，這可是實話吧？

116

喔，對了，我還把我的名字改成茱蒂了，所以往後請叫我茱蒂。

您永遠的，
茱蒂（原茱露莎‧亞伯特）

----

10 月 25 日

親愛的長腿叔叔：

萬歲！我加入籃球隊了。不過，茱莉亞‧潘鐸頓沒上！

我全身都是瘀傷。我好愛大學，一切正漸入佳境。

我知道我不該問您任何問題，可是我只有一件事想問。一個高挑、富有、慷慨，又討厭女生的男士，是長什麼樣子？

請回答這個問題。這對我很重要。

您的
茱蒂‧亞伯特

p. 34–35

12 月 19 日

親愛的長腿叔叔：

您始終未回答我的問題。您是禿頭嗎？我對您的模樣大致有一個想法，除了您的頭。我無法決定您是黑髮、白髮，還是銀灰色的頭髮。也許您根本沒有頭髮。

我畫了一張您的肖像。我覺得您長得像這樣：（附圖）您似乎就是個憤怒的老人。

我有好多書需要讀。我需要讀的書其他女生統統都讀過了。

耶誕假期下週就要開始了。只剩下我和另一個女生兩個會留在學校。我計畫整整三個星期的假期要念許多書。一定會很棒。

您永遠的，
茱蒂

附記：請告訴我您長得什麼樣子。要您的秘書
　　　拍一封電報，告知任一項答案：
　　　1. 史密斯先生頭很禿。
　　　或，2. 史密斯先生頭不禿。
　　　或，3. 史密斯先生有白髮。

p. 36–37

確切日期不明

親愛的長腿叔叔：

這裡在下雪，萬物覆蓋著一片白。

謝謝您的耶誕禮物。五枚金幣真是個大驚喜，尤其您已為我做了這麼多。

您想知道我買了什麼嗎？我買了一隻銀錶，這樣我就會永遠準時了，還有五百張黃色稿紙（以備我成為作家時使用），以及一本同義詞辭典（加強我的字彙）。

非常感謝您讓我有了這麼多的禮物。再過兩天假期就要結束了，見到大家一定會很開心，這裡已經變得有些寂寞。

謝謝您為我所做的一切。

愛您的，
茱蒂
附記：我希望您不介意我致上愛。我需要有人去愛，而您是我
　　　唯一認識的人。

p. 38–39

親愛的長腿叔叔：

　　首先，我有一些大好的消息。
茱露莎‧亞伯特已成為一名作家。我
的詩〈從我的塔樓〉將刊登在二月的
月刊上。我會寄給您一份。好棒吧？

　　我還做了許多其他的事。我學會
了如何溜冰。我現在可以溜圈圈也不
會跌倒。還有，在體育館，我可以從體育館的頂端，滑著繩子
下來，我還學會了翻過三呎六吋高的單槓。這動作起初很可
怕，但是現在我做所有動作都很輕鬆。

　　嗯，我還有一些壞消息。我希望您現在心情很好。我的數
學和拉丁文被當了。可是我現在有老師在個別指導這兩科。請
原諒我。我保證一定不會再被當。

p. 40–41 我學了許多其他的東西，還讀了十七部小說和許多篇
詩文。數學和拉丁文並不是一切！

您的，
茱蒂

本月焦點新聞

茱蒂學習溜冰
還有翻單槓
她收到兩張學科被當
但是她保證要用功讀書

親愛的長腿叔叔：

　　我剛收到莉佩特太太來的一封信。她告訴我，暑假期間我可以回孤兒院工作。我討厭約翰·格利爾之家。我寧願去死。

您最誠實的，
茱露莎·亞伯特

[第三章] 哲維少爺

`p. 46-47`

　　親愛的長腿叔叔：

　　這座校園在五月裡真美。繁花綻放，所有人都跑到戶外，享受美好的天氣。

　　我們快要考試了，可是沒有人去想它。暑假就快到了！我也好高興！今年夏天我會非常勤奮地工作，要成為一名很棒的作家。

　　我還有別的消息要告訴您。我曾跟一位非常和善的男士共度一些時光，一位非常高尚的男士。他是茱莉亞家的哲維斯·潘鐸頓先生，他是她高個子的叔叔。

　　他來城裡洽公，決定來看望茱莉亞，可是她在上課，所以他請我陪他去逛逛校園。

p. 48–49 他一點也不像潘鐸頓家族的其他人。他是那麼的和善，身材又高又瘦，掛著有趣的微笑。

我跟他在一起感覺非常的舒服自在。我們走遍了校園，然後在大學餐廳喝茶，吃馬芬麵包配橘子醬，還有冰淇淋和蛋糕，度過了最美好的時光。

但之後他為了趕搭火車便離開了。茱莉亞很氣我佔用了他一整個時間。

他似乎是個十分富有的叔叔。而今天早晨，茱莉亞、莎莉和我自己，都收到了驚喜。每人一盒巧克力！

我真的再也不覺得像個孤兒了！

您永遠的，
茱蒂

p. 50–51

6 月 9 日

親愛的長腿叔叔：

我的考試終於都結束了。

我好興奮要在一座農場上度過三個月。萬分謝謝您遣我去那兒，而不是回孤兒院。

我以前從未去過農場，但我知道我會喜歡細柳湖。

您永遠的，
茱蒂

親愛的長腿叔叔：

　　我在農場裡了，這是個最最美妙、天堂般的地方。

　　我真的喜歡森波夫婦，他們是農場主人。

　　今晚我們吃了火腿、雞蛋、餅乾、蜂蜜、果凍蛋糕、派餅、醃黃瓜、乳酪，還喝了茶。我們都聊了好多。

　　現在是晚上八點半。我等不及明天要去探索了。

晚安，
茱蒂

---

p. 52–53

7 月 12 日

親愛的長腿叔叔：

　　您的祕書怎麼知道細柳湖？這真奇怪，因為哲維斯‧潘鐸頓先生從前是這座農場的主人。真是太巧了！

　　後來他把農場送給了森波太太，她曾經擔任他的護士。她經常談到「哲維少爺」從前是多麼貼心。

　　我的工作是撿雞蛋。昨天，我想要撿拾雞蛋，結果從一根橫木上摔了下來。

　　這裡有好多雞、豬和火雞，還有五隻小牛，我把牠們命名為秀維亞、莎莉、茱莉亞、茱蒂和長腿叔叔。我希望您不介意。長腿叔叔長得像這樣：

　　我很樂於送您一些我做的甜甜圈。

您永遠的，
茱蒂

p. 54–55

9 月 25 日

親愛的長腿叔叔：

　　我終於是個大二生了。上個禮拜五我回到學校。離開細柳湖我非常難過，但是回到熟悉的地方感覺很好。

　　這裡有了一些改變。我跟莎莉和茱莉亞是室友了，我們各自有自己的小套房，並共用一間書房。

　　今年莎莉要競選班長。我認為她會當選。

　　我也開始研讀化學了。我對它還是一知半解。這是一門很特別的科目。

　　我正在學習好多東西，叔叔，這一切多虧了您。

摯愛您的孤兒，

J·亞伯特

[第四章] 獨立的茱蒂

p. 58–59

3 月 24 日

親愛的長腿叔叔：

　　太多好事發生在我身上了。我確信我不應得這一切。我有天大的好消息！我贏得了月刊每年舉辦的短篇小說比賽。

　　獎金有二十五元，而且是屬於我的。我仍舊無法置信。

　　更特別的是，通常得獎者都是四年級生，可是我只是個二年級生。說不定我最終會成為一個成功的作家。

p. 60–61 我還有別的大好消息。下週五我和茱莉亞、莎莉要去紐約，我們會住旅館還要去購物。

　　週六，我們將跟「哲維少爺」一起上劇院看《哈姆雷特》。我對此行興奮得難以入眠。

　　這將是我頭一次住旅館和上劇院看戲。我興奮得頭都暈了。

　　我真心期待去看這齣戲，尤其因為我們在課堂上研讀過，而且我熟知所有的台詞。

您永遠的，
茱蒂

p. 62–63

4 月 7 日

親愛的長腿叔叔：

　　我在紐約了！我所見到的每件事物都令我感到驚異。一切是那麼的奇妙，但同時又是那麼的令人迷惑。

　　我無法向您鉅細靡遺地描述，但是我猜想您已經知道了，畢竟您是住在紐約的。

　　茱莉亞和我今天去購物。我看見了最最漂亮的帽子，而茱莉亞試了好多頂，最後她買了最可愛的兩頂。我覺得，只要她想買就能買下任何帽子，不用擔心花多少錢，實在讓人驚愕。

p. 64–65 週六下午我們也跟哲維少爺碰了面。他帶我們去了一間非常高雅的餐廳。

　　我點了魚，但是不知道該用哪一支叉子。我不小心用錯了叉子，但是侍者非常好心，給了我另一支。

　　用餐之後，我們去看戲。這齣戲著實令人驚歎。我依舊記得每個細節。男女演員都棒極了。喔！還有一件事！哲維少爺送給我們一人一束美麗的鮮花，有鈴蘭和紫羅蘭。

　　他真是個最和善的男士了，對吧？因為他的關係，我開始越來越喜歡男人了。

愛您的，
茱蒂

p. 66–67

5 月 4 日

親愛的長腿叔叔：

　　上週六我們舉行了運動日。活動一開始是一項歡欣鼓舞的遊行，但是莎莉和我不在遊行隊伍中，我們正等待參加我們的競賽項目。

　　您猜怎麼著？我們都贏了！莎莉贏了撐竿跳高，而我贏了 50 碼短跑（8 秒）。

　　整個過程非常刺激，一天結束，我們都感覺好痛快。那天晚上大家都很疲憊，我們都早早上床就寢。

我永遠愛您，
茱蒂

p. 68–69

6 月 4 日

親愛的叔叔：

　　這陣子我正忙著讀書準備考試，明天就考了。

　　天氣很好，讓人在室內待不住，不過我還是要繼續苦讀。

　　考試一結束我們就放假了，真讓人迫不及待，您猜得到這個假期我打算做什麼嗎？

　　去細柳湖？去莎莉家和她的家人一起過暑假？都不是，我要去海邊，當一個女孩和她妹妹的家庭教師，我要教她們英文和拉丁文，每個月可以賺到五十元！

　　請不要反對我的計畫。多虧了您，我漸漸變得非常獨立。

　　希望您有個美好的夏季，叔叔。

您永遠的，
　茱蒂

p. 70–71

6 月 10 日

親愛的長腿叔叔：

　　我寫這封信給您實在很難下筆。

　　您給了我一個絕好的機會，但我覺得今年夏天開始供養自己是我的責任，而不是讓您來送我去歐洲。

　　對於這件事我感受非常強烈，不過，您能給我這樣的一個機會，真是好心。

　　我正要將這封信付郵時，遇見了哲維少爺。他也邀請我去歐洲。

　　他說，那是我的教育中很重要的一環。我差點兒答應了，但是有一點阻止了我。

　　他幾乎是想要強迫我去，我拒絕被迫去做任何事，我想要獨立自主作出自己的決定。

　　為回報您的仁善，我會成為一個睿智獨立的女人。

　　您永遠的，
　　茱蒂

[第五章] 意外的真相

p. 76-77

6 月 19 日

親愛的長腿叔叔：

　　您能相信這件事嗎？我不相信。
我終於完成了大學學業，拿到了學位。

　　真謝謝您送給我的那束玫瑰，我抱著它走在畢業生的行列中。

　　我現在在細柳湖，除了寫書無所事事。哲維少爺八月要來細柳湖，我希望您也會來，但是我知道那是絕不會發生的。

茱蒂・亞伯特
文學士

7 月 24 日

親愛的長腿叔叔：

　　我度過了一個十分美好的夏天，我一直盡我所能寫作，只希望每天都能更長一些，那樣的話我就可以寫得更多。

　　這將是一本不折不扣的小說，叔叔。我對這本書充滿了興奮。

　　在細柳湖這裡，我有絕佳的工作場所，我擁有世上最美的景致、許許多多的食物、一張舒適的床鋪和完全滿足我所需的紙和墨水。

　　我想我是世界上最幸運的女孩了。

仍舊希望與您見面的，
茱蒂

---

9 月 19 日

親愛的叔叔：

　　我需要您就一個相當嚴肅的問題給予指點，我寧願跟您見面來談。

　　我擔心您的秘書會閱讀這封信，而我想要保密此事。請讓我去見您。此刻我非常不快樂。

茱蒂

p. 80–81

10 月 3 日

親愛的長腿叔叔：

　　我剛收到您捎來的消息。聽到您臥病，我好難過。但願我拿我的問題煩擾您之前，已經知道此事了。

　　我會在這封信中把我的問題告訴您，但是請您閱畢就把信燒了。不過，在告訴您之前，我（隨信）寄上一張一千元的支票。我賣掉了我的小說。

　　如果您收下這張支票，對我而言會是意義重大。我欠您的已經太多了，這輩子我只能用我的情感和感激來回報。這只是稍稍表示我對您的感念。

　　我的問題是這樣的。您知道我一直深深喜愛您，可是現在有另一個男士我更為喜愛。他是哲維少爺。

p. 82–83 我知道您不認識他，可是我但願您認識。他是那麼的仁善寬大，我們在一起相處得非常好。

　　我們總是為了同樣的事發笑。當我沒有跟他在一起時，我對他的思念更甚於世上他人。

　　您可曾愛過什麼人？除非您愛過，否則無法了解我的感受。

　　我真心喜愛他，可是我已拒絕嫁給他。我無法告訴他我是個孤兒。而且我覺得，像我這樣的人沒資格嫁入他那樣的家族。

　　如果他娶了我，他會後悔的，我永遠開不了口向他解釋我的理由。

　　這是大約兩個月前的事。從那以後我就一直心碎著，我未曾收到他的一絲消息。但是茉莉亞告訴我，他感染了肺炎，病得很重。我猜想他非常不快樂。您認為我應該怎麼做？

非常迷惘的茱蒂

p. 84–85

10 月 6 日

最親愛的長腿叔叔：

　　我好興奮終於有機會跟您見面了。下週三下午四點半！我不會忘記的。

　　我已去過紐約三次了，所以我應該能知道怎麼走。我真不敢相信我就要和您見面了。

　　長久以來我一直在猜想您，感覺您幾乎不像是真實的。謝謝您在身體不適時，還讓我去看望您。

摯愛地，
茱露莎

星期四早晨

我最親愛的哲維－長腿叔叔－潘鐸頓－史密斯少爺：

　　這些日子我幾乎難以成眠，因為我是如此快樂又興奮。然而，您病得這麼重，我感到好難過。請快快康復。

　　我擔心昨天發生的事只是我在作夢。我們只相聚了三十分鐘，但是我會記得每一個點點滴滴。

p. 86–87 相較於昨天早晨離開細柳湖的那個女孩，現在的我是很不同了。

　　昨天我一大早就起身，就著燭光吃了早餐，搭火車赴紐約。

　　從頭到尾，我都在跟自己唱著：「妳就要見到長腿叔叔了。」

　　我去到您的府邸，可是我太害怕，幾乎不敢進去。我走進您家時，您的總管待我非常和善。我在會客室中興奮地等候。而後，您的總管引我進入您的房間。

房間光線相當昏暗，所以一開始我看不太清楚。我先是注意到壁爐裡的火。我望過去，看見一把偌大的扶手椅。一位男士坐在那兒，靠著許多枕墊，蓋著好多毯子。我再仔細一看，才恍然發覺那是您。

p. 88–89 我以為那是叔叔開的玩笑。就在那一刻，您笑了出來，問道：「我親愛的茱蒂，難道妳沒猜到我就是長腿叔叔？」

當下我一句話也說不出來，太多事情在我腦海中掠過。我想到了許許多多可以透露給我叔叔就是您的線索。

我現在該怎麼稱呼您？叔叔？哲維斯？哲維？請告訴我。

我們的三十分鐘相聚過得太快了。我想要待久一點，但是您的醫生不准許。

返回細柳湖的路程真是一段奇異之旅。一路上我始終處於恍惚中。但是我感覺好幸福。

我好想念您，但是我知道我們很快就會相聚。現在我們彼此相屬了。我感到幸福無比，因為我終於屬於某個人了。我會時時盡我之力帶給您幸福。

我永遠是您的，
茱蒂

附記：我從未寫過情書，可是卻知道怎麼寫，這真是奇怪，不是嗎？

Answers

P. 26

(A) ❶ respectful ❷ rude ❸ have, written

(B) ❶ F ❷ T ❸ F ❹ T

P. 27

(C) ❶ (c) ❷ (c)

(D) ❶ was finished ❷ kept ❸ looked
❹ watched ❺ heard

P. 42

(A) ❶ - ⓒ ❷ - ⓔ ❸ - ⓐ ❹ - ⓕ
❺ - ⓓ ❻ - ⓑ

(B) ❶ (b) ❷ (c)

P. 43

(C) ❶ T ❷ F ❸ T ❹ F ❺ T

(D) ❸ → ❻ → ❶ → ❺ → ❹ → ❷

P. 56

(A) ❶ F ❷ T ❸ F ❹ T

(B) ❶ I used to play the piano every day.
❷ There used to be a tall tree here (instead of a tall building).

P. 57

(C) ❶ (b) ❷ (a)

(D) ❶ secretary ❷ coincidence
❸ nurse ❹ beam

P. 72

(A) ❶ - ⓑ ❷ - ⓒ ❸ - ⓔ ❹ - ⓐ ❺ - ⓓ

P. 73

(B) ❶ T ❷ F ❸ T ❹ F ❺ F

(C) ❶ to post ❷ has invited ❸ to be forced

P. 90

A **1** - d **2** - a **3** - e **4** - c **5** - f **6** - b

B **1** if **2** Unless **3** so **4** When

P. 91

C **2** → **3** → **4** → **1** → **5**

D **1** problem **2** deeply **3** another **4** wish

P. 108

A **1** She is an orphan, but she is funny and talented. —**Judy**
2 She is a good friend of Judy, and she runs for the class president. —**Sallie**
3 She is from a very wealthy family. She can buy anything she wants. —**Julia**
4 He is a tall and rich gentleman. He dislikes girls but Judy is an exception. —**Daddy-Long-Legs**
5 He is gentle and generous. He spends nice time with Judy. —**Master Jervie**

B **1** amazed **2** furnished **3** original **4** bruises **5** bald **6** secretary, private

P. 109

C **1** Why didn't Jerusha like Julia Pendleton? (c)
2 How did Jerusha imagine her benefactor look like? (a)
3 Why did Jerusha refuse to go to Europe with Mr. Pendleton? (b)

D **1** I have been very busy these days - c
2 I am so sorry - b
3 I feel that someone like me - a

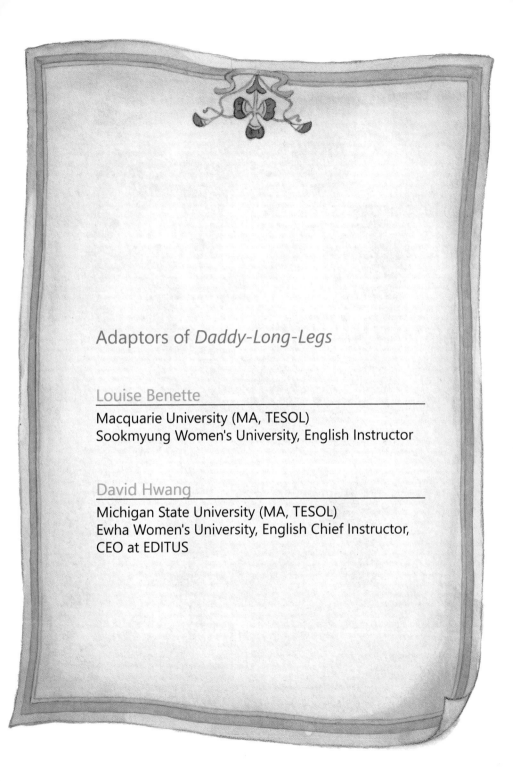

Adaptors of *Daddy-Long-Legs*

Louise Benette

Macquarie University (MA, TESOL)
Sookmyung Women's University, English Instructor

David Hwang

Michigan State University (MA, TESOL)
Ewha Women's University, English Chief Instructor,
CEO at EDITUS

長腿叔叔【二版】
Daddy-Long-Legs

作者 _ 珍・韋伯斯特
　　　（Jean Webster）
改寫 _ Louise Benette / David Hwang
插圖 _ An Ji-Yeon
翻譯 / 編輯 _ 黃鈺云
作者 / 故事簡介翻譯 _ 王采翎
校對 _ 王采翎
封面設計 _ 林書玉
排版 _ 葳豐／林書玉
播音員 _ Rebecca Kelly / Michael Blunk
製程管理 _ 洪巧玲
發行人 _ 周均亮
出版者 _ 寂天文化事業股份有限公司
電話 _ +886-2-2365-9739
傳真 _ +886-2-2365-9835
網址 _ www.icosmos.com.tw
讀者服務 _ onlineservice@icosmos.com.tw
出版日期 _ 2019年11月 二版一刷（250201）
郵撥帳號 _ 1998620-0 寂天文化事業股份有限公司

國家圖書館出版品預行編目資料

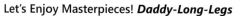

長腿叔叔 / Jean Webster 原著 ; Louise
Benette, David Hwang 改寫 . -- 二版 . -- 臺北市 :
寂天文化 , 2020.01　面 ;　公分
譯自 : Daddy-long-legs

ISBN 978-986-318-877-3(25K 平裝附光碟片)

874.59　　　　　　　　　　　108022343